The Mosts

Also by Melissa Senate

THEODORA TWIST

The Mosts

Melissa Senate

Delacorte Press

Copyright © 2010 by Melissa Senate

All rights reserved. Published in the United States by Delacorte Press,
an imprint of Random House Children's Books, a division of
Random House, Inc., New York.

Delacorte Press is a registered trademark and the colophon is a trademark of
Random House, Inc.

Visit us on the Web! www.randomhouse.com/teens

Educators and librarians, for a variety of teaching tools, visit us at
www.randomhouse.com/teachers

Library of Congress Cataloging-in-Publication Data
Senate, Melissa.
The Mosts / Melissa Senate.
p. cm.
Summary: After a summer makeover, Madeline begins dating one of the
most popular boys at her Maine high school, but when he moves to
California, she fears for both her status and her relationship.
ISBN 978-0-385-73303-8 (trade pbk: alk. paper) — ISBN 978-0-385-90323-3
(lib. bdg.) — ISBN 978-0-375-89657-6 (e-book)
[1. Popularity—Fiction. 2. Interpersonal relations—Fiction. 3. Dating (Social
customs)—Fiction. 4. Identity—Fiction. 5. High schools—Fiction.
6. Schools—Fiction. 7. Maine—Fiction.] I. Title.
PZ7.S4666Mo 2010
[Fic]—dc22
2009026226

The text of this book is set in 12-point Garamond.

Book design by Trish Parcell

Printed in the United States of America

10 9 8 7 6 5 4 3 2 1

First Edition

For my dear friend
Heidi Wartenberg Calvo-Cruz Cinicolo Caren,
whom I was lucky to meet
my first day of high school.
(You have a lot of names,
but you'll alway be just Hoodles to me.)

THE LISTS

THE MOSTS
(official list, printed in the yearbook)

Most Popular

Most Beautiful

Most Stylish

Most Hot

Most Likely to Rule the World One Day

Most Hilarious

Most Brainy

Class Couple

THE MOST NOTS
(underground list, voted on by secret committee
and handed out the last week of school)

Most in Need of an Extreme Makeover

Most in Need of a Therapist

Most in Need of Basic Grooming

Most in Need of a Stylist

Most Nerdy

Most Not Cool

Most in Need

Chapter 1

For two weeks, I asked everyone I met if they thought long-distance relationships worked. My friends all said yes, yes, yes. Absolutely. "Because when you're totally in love, that's all that matters," they insisted.

My parents and my older sister, Sabrina, who knows nothing about guys or love, said anything was possible, but "I don't think so."

Ms. Fingerman, my favorite teacher at Freeport Academy, where I'm a sophomore (for six more weeks), said a romance had once both begun and ended during her first-period English class. And then she quoted some sad, negative poetry about doomed love.

Then there were the strangers I consulted. Random store clerks and people on street corners downtown all said something to the effect that

"Most relationships can't handle a distance of more than twenty minutes. People get lazy. And their eyes wander. Like to the next desk or cubicle or seat on the bus." The waitress at Yum's, where my friends and Thom and I spent most of our free time because of their decadent low-fat fudge muffins and no table minimums, told me that her Colby College–bound boyfriend had promised they'd be together forever, and he'd dumped her after a month for a girl in his philosophy class. And Colby College was only an hour away from Freeport.

So did I believe my friends? Or everyone else?

"Believe *me*," Thom said, his gorgeous green eyes so intense that I did believe him. For a minute.

And then tears began pricking the backs of my own eyes.

Thom, my boyfriend of two years, was leaving. Moving from the coast of Maine to sunny Southern California, where it never snowed (or rained). Going far, far away in minutes.

We stood in the shade of the calves' barn on my parents' dairy farm, the warm May sunshine slanting light on the dark, hay-strewn cement floor. A cute black and white calf named Hermione (my stepfather, Mac, named all that spring's calves after Harry Potter characters) stood in her corral just a few feet from us, peering at us with her big black eyes. She kept nudging us with her pink nose, which meant she wanted her milk. We fed calves with a giant baby bottle, which was the only thing on the farm I liked doing. Feeding the calves was the job of the high school interns who worked on the farm for school credit; one of them was already here that morning, eight a.m. on a Sunday. Crazy. It wasn't the most romantic place for a goodbye, for a last kiss. But the calves' barn was where we'd met. Where Thom Geller had first noticed me two years before. I wanted to bury him under a huge pile of hay and keep him here forever.

"We are *not* breaking up, Madeline," he said for the tenth time in ten minutes. He cupped my face with his hands and kissed me on the nose.

Which made me burst into tears.

I'd been stocking up on Visine for the past two weeks. Tears streamed down my face at the most random times, even when I wasn't thinking about my boyfriend leaving. Like the moment I woke up in the morning, before I even remembered. And in the middle of English class (which was why I'd asked Ms. Fingerman her opinion of long-distance relationships, then wished I hadn't), since we were reading *Romeo and Juliet,* the most tragic teen love story of all. And while walking down the halls of Freeport Academy with my friends, who would immediately pull me into hugs, with "Just because Thom's moving to California—where girls probably wear bikinis to class—doesn't mean you guys are breaking up."

Thom himself had been saying that ever since he'd found out that his dad had been transferred from his big-deal corporate job in Maine to a bigger, better one in California. But California was across the country from Maine, three time zones away. When I'd be eating gloppy tuna sandwiches in the caf, Thom would be hitting the snooze button on his alarm clock for the third time. Our lives would be completely different at completely different times. Out of sync.

"We'll call, text, IM, e-mail, everything," he said, tipping up my chin. "We're us. We'll always be us, Madeline."

I really wanted to believe that. I was crazy about him. Thom was my first boyfriend. The first guy I'd ever had a crush on, the first guy I'd ever kissed. The first (and only) guy who had ever told me I was beautiful—and way before anyone would have looked at me and said I was even pretty. Thom liked me *before*—before I went from blah farm girl with no friends to the most popular girl at Freeport Academy. He liked *me*.

"Promise?" I asked. "Even though I heard girls really do wear bikinis to class in L.A.?"

He smiled that smile, complete with popping dimple in his left cheek, that had left me speechless the first time he had ever spoken to me. "No girl in a bikini could ever compare to you, Madeline. I've seen you in a bikini."

Okay, he was making me feel better. Making me believe him. Maybe this *could* work out. "You think three thousand miles can touch us?" he asked, pulling me into a hug. "No way."

Yum, he felt so good. I loved his hugs. And because we only had a few more minutes before his mom would pull up the drive and honk the horn on the big green Subaru, I didn't remind him about Carlie and Johanna, my former best friends from New York, where I'd lived before my mom had married Mac and followed her bliss to buy a farm in Maine. The day I'd said goodbye to Carlie and Johanna, we'd sobbed and hugged and written *MCJ BFF!* in hearts on our arms with red Sharpies. Our e-mails and texts lasted as long as the supposedly permanent marker: three weeks. Day by day, the red faded, and finally I didn't even realize it wasn't there anymore.

"I'm going to miss you so much," I said, looking up at him. Thom was tall, almost six feet, and he wasn't even sixteen yet, not for another two months. "I just can't believe I'm not going to see your face every day."

"Ditto," he said, and held on to me. "This is where we met, remember?"

Like I would ever forget. I'd been in the calves'
barn after school that day two years ago, sitting on
a tiny stool in Prince Harry's small wooden corral.
(That spring Mac had named the calves after mem-
bers of the British royal family.) I didn't mind the
calves' barn the way I minded—okay, *hated*—the
farm in general. I liked the cute, sweet little calves.
They were a comfort to me when I was upset about
something. That day, I had worked up the nerve
to say hello to Annie Haywood, the funniest girl in
school. Earlier, she'd told a joke that made me laugh
every time I thought about it. I'd planned to tell
her that, but when I walked up to her, she looked at
me for one second, as though a fly had buzzed
near her ear, then turned around and started talking
to someone else, blowing me off completely.

I'd looked down at my boxy royal-blue New
England Aquarium T-shirt, with its giant comical octopus, and my no-name jeans and stupid, hopeless
white sneakers and known that Annie and her
friends would never talk to me. I didn't look like
them and I didn't know how to look like them. Or
act like them.

So I was feeling like a real nobody when Thom
Geller poked his head in, saw me feeding Prince
Harry with the baby bottle, and said, "That is *so*
cool. Can I try that?"

Thom was one of the most popular guys at

school, boyfriend of a glittering blond cheerleader named Morgan. But he was more than that. He was the boy whose face, whose voice, whose smile had made me stop dead in my tracks when I'd seen him on my first day of eighth grade. Thom was smart and funny and nice, but he never once looked my way, not even when I stared at him so hard I was sure everyone noticed.

Thom lived a few houses down from me, which in Maine could easily—and did—mean a mile away. That day, he'd ridden his bike over to see his friend Sam, who'd recently started interning at the farm twice a week. He'd spoken to me for the first time. Ever.

I'd jumped. I hadn't heard him ride up, hadn't seen him standing there, watching me.

And since Sam was still working, Thom stayed with me in the small corral, just four feet by four feet and fenced in on all sides. Me, the *before* me, in my octopus T-shirt and dirty Wellies, the rubber boots you wore unless you wanted your shoes caked with dirt and cow poop.

Thom watched the way I fed Prince Harry for a while and then I gave Thom the bottle. "Is this right?" he asked. When I told him that he was doing it perfectly, that Prince Harry really seemed to like him, the smile Thom shot me, complete with that dimple popping, almost undid me right there.

Then we both just sat on our stools, watching Prince Harry suck. Thom asked what kind of cow he was, and I explained the different kinds of dairy cows and told him that we raised Holsteins—the black and white ones—and had our own milk and dairy products business, complete with a cute label that my mom had designed. It said AnnaBeth's Farm Fresh milk, cheese, and ice cream and had an illustration of a Holstein calf that my sister had drawn. (She's a decent artist; I give her that.) I surprised myself by how much I knew, especially since we'd only lived on the farm since the previous August, not even a year then, and I couldn't stand the place. I figured I'd picked up a lot of info by being forced to listen to farm talk at dinner. Plus if I wanted to talk to my mom, I usually had to follow her around the farm as she did her work on the milking machines. No one with a working dairy farm milked by hand anymore, well, unless you had maybe like two cows. So I learned a lot by just watching.

Thom really listened to me, looked into my eyes as I talked, and asked questions he seemed impressed I could answer, like what the heck a heifer was (a female cow who hadn't yet had a calf).

And that was when Thom said it, just turned and stared at me for a minute and said it: "You have the prettiest face."

I almost fainted. It took me a few minutes to say, "Thanks, so do you," which made me feel like a moron, but he laughed. And suddenly, there in the doorway was his friend Sam, who said something cute like "See? I told you working on a farm was fun." Thom looked at me one last time and said thanks and bye, and he was gone.

At school the next day, I walked past him and tried to catch his eye, but he didn't even look my way, didn't see me. A week or so later, as we were walking out of history class, he said, "Oh, hey, you're the girl from Sam's farm." And before I could get out more than a "yeah," the glittering, popular girls had surrounded him and pulled him away. And then he just seemed to forget me and look through me—if he looked my way at all—as everyone else did.

When school ended, I went to Rome to stay with my aunt Darcy (my dad's sister) for all of August. That trip changed my life.

I came back just a week before my freshman year started. Thom had ridden to the farm to pick up Sam after his shift one day, and he didn't even recognize me when I walked out of the main house. He'd stared at me in my pencil skirt, textured knee-high boots, and fitted white T-shirt, my hair pulled back in a messy bun, a delicate little scarf tied around my neck. Then he said hi and asked if I was friends with the girl who lived here. I laughed the mysterious yet friendly and throaty way I'd seen Italian girls laugh and told him that I *was* the girl who lived here, that I'd just come back from a month in Rome. And he said, "Wow, you've really changed." He asked if I wanted to go to a movie, and a week later, when school started, we were a couple. And I was an entirely different girl.

Honk!

No. It couldn't be time yet. But when we turned to look out the barn door, there was his mom at the wheel of the familiar green car. Mrs. Geller gave us a sympathetic smile and then turned to her husband, to give us privacy, I assumed.

Thom pulled me farther behind the door and kissed me like it was our last kiss, which both made me happy and made me start crying again.

"I love you," he said, looking right into my eyes, and there were tears in his own. I'd never seen Thom Geller cry before. Ever.

He squeezed my hand and then ran down the path to the car.

I stood between the open double doors of the barn, two of our huge ducks waddling past me. Tears streamed down my face as Thom took one last look and then got into the car. Suddenly all I had of Thom Geller was his face in the back window, his hand against the glass. And because of the stupid hill on Flying Point Road, that face was out of view in four seconds.

"I love you too," I called out.

I went back inside the calves' barn, because I was crying hard. I didn't want to hear my mom or Mac or my sister tell me that I'd be okay, which was what they'd been doing for the past two weeks. Why would I be okay? I went into Hermione's corral and sat down on the tiny wooden stool and cried into her short, stubby fur.

That was when I heard a sound like something metal crashing against the floor. I turned around and there was Elinor Espinoza, one of the farm interns. She looked terrified.

"Um, I . . . w-was just . . . ," she stammered, looking at me, then down at the ground, her face bright red. She tugged at her wildly curly-frizzy, square-shaped dark hair.

I jumped up. "Were you back there the whole time?"

"I . . . It's . . . You guys came in kind of suddenly and I was spreading out clean hay and then I didn't know if I should interrupt to say I was there, and . . ."

I just stared at her, but then the tears came back and I ran out of the barn and into the main house. I was halfway up the stairs when my mom saw me.

She looked like a lumberjack in her overalls and work boots, her long, graying brown hair in two pigtailed braids. "Oh, Maddie, honey, did Thom just go? I know it hurts. How about we take you out for breakfast? Eggs, bacon, the works."

Like I could eat. "I just need to be alone."

She nodded. "You're probably going to cry for a while. I'll come check on you later with some mint chocolate chip, just in case you're in the mood."

I ran to my room and closed the door, and of course the first thing I saw was my computer's screen saver, a shot of the official school award declaring Madeline Echols and Thomas Geller Freshman Class Couple last year.

The end of school was just six weeks away. That meant everyone would be voting for Most This and Most That and Class Couple. Thom and I wouldn't be in the running for Sophomore Class Couple.

And according to most of the general population of Freeport, Maine, as of two minutes earlier, Thom and I weren't a couple anymore at all.

Chapter 2

I was playing What's Thom Doing Now? when the phone rang. For the past hour, I'd been looking at the clock and deciding where he must be and what he might be doing. Eight-fifteen a.m.: probably hitting the Portland city limits on I-295. Eight-twenty: arriving at the Portland jetport. Eight-forty-five: sitting in the waiting area, reading *Spin* magazine (Thom loved alternative music) or playing his Nintendo DS or looking at pictures of me on his cell phone.

I bolted up from my bed, where I'd spent that hour staring at the ceiling, and grabbed my cell from the bedside table. Thom. I couldn't flip it open fast enough.

"Hey, we're at the airport. I just wanted to tell you I already miss you."

That was a good sign. But then again, he hadn't even left the state.

"Me too. So, so much."

"But you'll come out for your dad's wedding in a few weeks and it'll be like we're not apart."

My father lived in California, just twenty minutes from Santa Anita, where Thom was moving. In three and a half weeks, I was going to his wedding—his third—and would get to see Thom again. Not that I'd even received an invitation yet—or heard from my dad about arranging airline tickets. I'd called him three times in the past two weeks to ask if he'd booked the flights for me and Sabrina. He'd said that he'd get on it, that of course he wanted his baby girls at his wedding.

But nothing.

Three and a half weeks. Felt like forever, but it wasn't. "I can't wait," I whispered, fighting back more tears.

"Me too. Hey, I have to go, my mom's waving me over. I'll text you later, okay?"

Two minutes later, my phone rang again. But it wasn't Thom. It was my best friend, Caro.

A creepy, scary, slightly nausea-producing feeling slunk inside my stomach. I wasn't in the mood to talk to Caro, especially now. Things had been a little weird between us the past couple of weeks, ever since Thom had announced he was moving.

I took a deep breath and answered the phone.

"Are you okay? Did he leave yet? I'll totally

14

come over to the stinky, gross farm if you're not okay. And not even because Sam might be there."

"I'm not okay," I admitted, surprised by Caro's sacrifice. "And Sam's not working today."

"I'll be over in ten minutes with everyone," she said, and hung up.

I sat down at the window seat that overlooked the pasture and the rise of hills where the herd was grazing. Caro Alexander, the reigning queen of Freeport Academy, was complicated. She hated the smell of the farm and would never hang out at my house if the very hot Sam Fray didn't intern twice a week and come on Saturdays for no credit. Caro had gone as far as to buy cute Burberry rubber boots to change into for crossing from the parking lot to the house. (The dirt driveway was a mudfest and used by people and chickens and turkeys and ducks, plus the usual variety of cats and dogs, so there was animal poop everywhere.) But she was so grossed out by the sight of livestock that she only came over twice. That was how much she hated the farm. Still, I was surprised Caro didn't show up more often in one of her skintight outfits and pink plaid Wellies just to be with Sam. She had given the farm a second chance, thinking she could feed a calf from a bottle and hook Sam the way I'd hooked Thom, but the calf had nudged her arm with its wet nose and she was grossed out permanently.

That she was coming over this early on a Sunday, when Sam wasn't even here to flirt with, said a lot about our friendship.

Caro *wanted* Sam. They'd kissed, sort of hooked up a little at parties, but he always pulled away from her before crossing some kind of "okay, we're together now" line, and never asked her out. She didn't get it, since every other guy at school lusted after her. Caro Alexander was girl perfection, neither too tall nor too short, slender yet curvy, and a C-cup chest. Then there was the angelic face, the long, swirly light blond hair, the round blue eyes—so slightly and expertly made up you weren't even sure she wore makeup—the glossy pink bow lips. Even male teachers stared at her before they caught themselves. She was without question stare-at-her beautiful. Hence voted Most Beautiful in the class poll since seventh grade.

"We're here!" I heard Fergie call from downstairs.

"And we have fat-free frozen yogurt!" Annie added. Yes, *that* Annie, the funny one.

"With fat-free hot fudge," Selena called up the stairs. "And Sprite Zero."

My friends were great. They were here when I needed them. And boy, did I need them right now.

I opened my door and there they were, four girls who, two years before, I never thought would ever talk to me, let alone turn into my best friends.

16

They were the Mosts of Freeport Academy. Caro Alexander, Most Beautiful. Fergie Ferragamo, Most Stylish. Annie Haywood, Most Hilarious (though sometimes I wanted to slap her). And Selena McFarland, Most Hot. And somehow I, Madeline Echols, had come out of nowhere to be named Most Popular last May in the freshman class polls. I was one of the Mosts. Though it wasn't official until last spring, I'd been in the clique from practically the first day of my freshman year. Thanks to Thom.

The creepy feeling returned. Lately I'd been wondering if these girls would be my friends at all if it hadn't been for Thom.

"You look so sad," Fergie said, fake pouting and running over in high-heeled sandals to hug me.

Fergie, whose nickname—everyone called her Fergie except her family—came from her very apt last name, Ferragamo (no relation to the couture designer, though), narrowly won back Most Stylish last year. She had lost it the year before to some artsy girl named Alanna, who had broken both legs and had very stylish shirt-coordinated cast covers made for each week. Fergie had been campaigning for this year's top prize since the school year had begun. She didn't think her real name—Mary Margaret— was appropriate for a stylin' girl, so she had ditched it the summer before seventh grade.

Fergie took her brush out of her huge purse and

hogged the mirror on the inside of my closet door to brush her chic auburn hair, which was secretly wildly curly-frizzy like Elinor Espinoza's, but had been Japanese-straightened and flat-ironed to perfection. Fergie had a killer bob, just past her chin, slightly A-line, which meant it was shorter in the back, and model-like bangs. Unlike me and Caro, Fergie was short, but she had a hot body. I was the only one of us who was practically flat-chested, but a trip to Victoria's Secret fixed that—as much as it could, anyway.

"Anyone would be sad with the stink of this place," Caro said, wrinkling her nose as she pulled something out of her leather messenger bag. She wore the pink plaid Wellies with supertight jeans tucked inside. "Guess what I did for you last night," she said, handing me something wrapped in bright pink paper with a bow on top.

"What's this?" I asked.

She smiled at me, those supposedly angelic blue eyes cool, though. I hated how she could manage that expression. "Open it," she said, sitting down on my bed and crossing her long legs. She took off her fitted ice-blue cardigan to reveal a microfiber tank top. She looked amazing, as always.

Fergie, Annie, and Selena crowded around me at the window seat, across from my bed. I unwrapped the glossy pink paper to find the Freeport Academy freshman class yearbook. Uh, I had one of these already.

"Open it to the pages with the little pink Post-its," Caro added.

I flipped to the first one. A pink Post-it arrow was on the page of kids whose last name began with A. The black-and-white photo of Reid Archer had a big red heart in marker around it. The next Post-it pointed to the same around James McNeil. There were six photos with giant hearts in total.

"I don't get it," Selena said, looking from me to Caro. She raked her hands through her long, shiny hair and made a quick braid, which fell apart in two seconds. Selena McFarland wasn't known for her brains, but she had a good heart and a killer body.

But to her credit, I didn't get it either. What were the hearts about?

"They're not in order," Caro said, as if that explained anything. "Reid's only first because he's alphabetical. But honestly, I'd go for James. He's hot and will likely be captain of the lacrosse team next year."

We all stared at her.

"Huh?" I said. "I thought you liked Sam."

"I didn't mean *I'd* go for James. I meant you should."

"Me? Why would I go for James or any guy? Thom and I didn't break up. He just spent a half

19

hour telling me we were *not* breaking up, that we could do this long-distance thing."

"Oh my god, that is so sweet," Annie said, applying a shimmery pink gloss in the mirror of a compact. She turned her attention from the mirror to me. "Do you think he really meant it?"

I really didn't like Annie. At all. But she was part of the group, and she mostly hung out with Selena—well, worshipped at her feet, really. Caro and Fergie and I were our own mini-clique within the group. Occasionally Annie made me laugh— and sent Selena and Fergie into hysterics—but there was always something snide and snarky to her humor. And of course I'd never quite forgiven her for the dis before I joined the group. She, like the other girls, had claimed to not even know I existed before I became one of them. *Madeline Echols? That's not even remotely familiar,* they'd all said. *And ours is a small school.*

"I'm sure he did," Fergie said. "Thom is madly in love with Madeline. They've been a couple for *two years.*"

I smiled at her. "I'm sure he did too. I know he did. And we're going to see each other in just three and a half weeks, when I fly out for my dad's wedding. After that, he can fly in or I can fly out every couple of months or something."

"Are you kidding? Airline tickets to California

cost a *fortune*." Annie giggled. "Oh, wait, Maddie will pay for her flight by selling eggs from her chicken coop and making her own stinky cheese." Caro shot her a look that said, *Uncool of you.* So of course Annie stopped laughing instantly. "I just mean that flying costs a lot. My family didn't even go to my uncle's graduation from Stanford Law School because it was so expensive."

Wait. This was making me feel better? This was cheering me up?

"Honey," Caro said, looking at me. "What I'm trying to say by the gift I gave you"—she pointed at the yearbook open on my lap to James's picture— "is that despite how much you like Thom, despite how much he likes you, you really do need to face cold, hard reality. He's *three thousand* miles away. In California. Where *every* girl looks like we do. But in bikinis. I'm sure you two will keep it going as long as you can—maybe until your dad's wedding. But honestly, you're going to hook up with some- one else and so is Thom. So I just circled the hottest guys to take his place."

I let out a very deep sigh. No. Reality or not, Thom said we weren't breaking up. *I* said we weren't breaking up. *We* said we weren't breaking up.

That was what mattered.

"No one's taking Thom's place," I said to Caro. "I'm not even remotely interested in other guys."

21

"This *second,* of course," she said. "I mean, your boyfriend of two years *just* left. But tomorrow morning at Freeport Academy, you're going to be considered single, Madeline. Guys are going to be asking you out. I've just done your weeding and vetting for you. If Reid asks you out before James, I'd stall him for a few days and wait for James."

Fergie nodded and took the yearbook off my lap. She flipped through the pink-marked pages. "They *are* the other hottest guys in school. Besides Sam and Tate."

"And Sam and Tate are totally off-limits," Selena said. "Because Sam is Caro's. And Tate is Fergie's."

Caro smiled. "That's very kind of you, Selena. But he's not mine yet."

Selena moved over to the mirror and began checking out her stomach to make sure it was flat enough. "Matter of time," she told Caro. "And it's understood no one can go for him while you want him. *I* drool over him," she said, thrusting out her 32D chest in her tight pink T-shirt. "But I'd *never.*"

"And I appreciate that," Caro said coolly.

Caro liked Annie and Selena, even though she referred to them as fringe Mosts. Caro had once said, "I'm funny and hot *and* everything else. They're just *one thing.*"

"Sam isn't like other guys," Caro said, moving

from my bed to the mirror and basically pushing Fergie and Selena out of the way. "He's not going to be attracted to *just* looks. But you're right. No one goes for Sam until I've figured out how to get him."

She didn't look at me while making that announcement. But she didn't have to. Everyone had noticed Sam watching me, staring at me, talking to me the past couple of weeks. I'd noticed for the past few months. Sam, with his sandy-blond hair and pale brown eyes, was *very* good-looking, very everything. And he was nice on top of it, in a way none of the other guys were. But ever since Thom had told us he was moving, I'd noticed Sam staring at me at lunch and at Yum's, where we all often hung out after school. And at the farm, three times a week.

Caro had noticed immediately—which accounted for the weirdness between us. Unspoken, unacknowledged weirdness. I'd tried to ignore it, because it was so far-fetched. I was into Thom and only Thom. And I'd long thought of Sam as Caro's. He'd never registered on my radar *that* way, even though he was amazingly cute. And nice. And easy to talk to. And always around, with something interesting to say.

Wait a minute. I glanced at Caro, at her reflection in the mirror. She didn't look at me, just adjusted her perfect jeans in her perfect boots.

Interesting. Caro had braved the stinky farm, no Sam and all, ostensibly to comfort me, but really to make sure I understood something: Sam was hers to hook.

As I said, Caro Alexander was complicated. Which meant she had her nice moments, her not-nice moments, and a confusing mix of the two, when you couldn't be sure if she was being nice or a total beyotch.

I would never forget the first time she talked to me, that very first day of ninth grade, when I'd walked into Freeport Academy hand in hand with Thom Geller. No one knew who I was. And so I was an overnight sensation, a new, cool It Girl who'd suddenly appeared in school like magic. Caro, in my homeroom, pointed at the chair next to hers when I walked in. And we left that class best friends. It sounds stupid, but it was true. We wrote notes back and forth all during homeroom, starting with *So you're with Thom Geller? He's hot. Love your shoes.*

And I wrote back that I was crazy about Thom and that I'd gotten the shoes in Rome, where I'd spent the summer (and where Caro had been twice), which led to more notes about how incredibly good-looking and romantic Italian boys were. Which led to who else I thought was cute at Freeport Academy. *Good, we have totally different types,* she wrote. *You like dark-haired guys. I like blonds.* Back then, she was going out with Andrew Auerman, who every girl lusted after and who later moved.

We walked out of homeroom together. Caro introduced me to Fergie and then Annie and Selena, and then all the other girls they deemed worthy—the other cheerleaders (Selena was one and so was Thom's ex-girlfriend, Morgan, who'd dumped Thom for a hot junior)—and that was that. I was in. And not just in with the popular girls—in with *everyone*. Becoming Most Popular had a lot to do with what I'd learned in Rome—about fashion, about food, about style, about European flair, about walking with a certain confidence—and giving other girls advice and showing them what I knew. That eyeliner should be applied to the top lids only—not the bottom. That sheer lipsticks were better for day than heavy mattes. That just the right type of little scarf around your neck could style up a plain white T-shirt. And that boxy cuts, whether shirts or sweaters, were not your friends. I helped with bangs. With shoes. With talking to guys and seeming mysterious, which every girl wanted to be. I was the go-to girl for just about everything. And come May of last year, I'd been voted Most Popular.

That seemed to suit Caro. She was the queen of Freeport Academy, but everyone was intimidated by her. She didn't expect to win Most Popular when most girls didn't dare even look her in the eye. So our friendship worked just fine.

The thing about Caro was that I liked her. There was a side of her that was real and deep and honest and compassionate. And our friendship had deepened when Andrew had broken up with her. I'd never seen Caro Alexander at anything less than the top of her game. And suddenly, she was heartbroken.

She'd cried for three days straight. I spent hours with her in her room, bringing her low-fat frozen yogurt and tissues and just listening. She was so sad that she couldn't summon any anger to do something vicious to Naomi Clark, Andrew's new girlfriend. She just asked over and over again, *Why her?* And all the studying of semigothy Naomi revealed nothing but that she had very large breasts for a thirteen-year-old and a penchant for wearing black tights. Caro started changing into Miracle Bras at school. Andrew then dumped Naomi for her, but then redumped Caro. Since Caro considered Naomi to be much less attractive than she was, she finally decided that Andrew's bad taste was such a turnoff that she got over him almost immediately.

Another thing Caro had done that I'd never forgotten: The day after Thom had asked me if we could be exclusive, Caro had had all the girls over to her house to celebrate. I still had the sparkly red lips keychain she'd given me as a present.

And there was the time Fergie's mom had been in the hospital with something weird and scary (something about blood platelets). For almost two weeks in ninth grade, Caro accompanied Fergie to visit her every day after school, sitting in the waiting room until Fergie came out of her mom's room, usually crying. I was there too, but it was Caro who wrote me notes or texted me every day with *hospital after school?*

Caro was smart and funny and she was very generous when she wasn't being mean. She'd opened her closet to me from day one. She knew all my secrets and was careful with them. Not that I had anything earth-shattering going on, but she knew *everything* and I never heard my secrets come out of Fergie's or Annie's or Selena's mouths.

And she trusted me with her secrets.

Like that when Michael Fage, who she'd been totally in love with the year before, had told her he'd dump her unless she had sex with him, she'd dumped him. He then moved on to Naomi Clark, and Caro finally knew what Naomi's secret was. Still, Caro cried her eyes out, and I was there with the tissues and the frozen yogurt again.

She'd been there for me. I'd been there for her.

But now what if she saw me as a threat?

Caro sat down on my bed. "Okay, so now that we're settled on who Madeline will be going for, will someone get me a Diet Coke?"

"I will!" Annie said, practically running out of the room and down the stairs. Most Hilarious wasn't a guy magnet the way the other Mosts were. Annie would do anything for Caro Alexander—to stay in the group.

I checked my cell phone to see if Thom had texted. He had. *XXXXXXX T.* I smiled, then shivered when I thought about what Caro had said. Did I have to face cold, hard reality about long-distance relationships? Or was she just being the mean, bitchy Caro who wanted to make sure I didn't go after the guy she wanted?

"You're *out,*" Caro said with a sneer as she applied pinkish red lip gloss in the ornate silver mirror on the inside of her locker door.

"*So* out," Fergie added, making a flicking motion at me with her fingers.

"Out, out, out," Annie and Selena chanted, coming closer and closer. "We—and that means *all* of us—were only your friends because you were Thom's girlfriend," they said in unison. "You were a nobody before and you're a nobody now."

"*Buh-bye,*" Caro said in my face, and then she

laughed and walked away, her hangers-on following single file after making that Fergie finger-flick at me.

I bolted up. I was alone in my room, in my bed. I glanced at the glowing digital clock on my nightstand: 1:43 a.m.

A dream. It had been just a very bad dream.

My heart was booming so loudly in my chest I figured my mom would come running in at any minute. After I stopped hyperventilating, I lay back down and stared at the ceiling.

That was some nightmare.

And it had spooked me.

Chapter 3

"Um, Madeline?"

I was face-deep in my locker, staring at a picture of Thom. According to his last text, he was heading to his new high school and hoping everyone would be great like at Freeport Academy. He didn't have anything to worry about. A gorgeous, likeable athlete like Thom would have no problem fitting in.

"Madeline? Can I . . . talk to you about something?"

I knew that squeaky voice. Elinor Espinoza.

I took one last look at Thom's green eyes, at his dark hair falling over his forehead, at that delicious dimple in his left cheek. I said my usual silent prayer that he was thinking of me right then and not talking to some beautiful tanned girl in a string bikini at Santa Anita Academy. I was pretty sure all girls in California were both tanned and beautiful and got to wear bikini tops to school.

With a sigh, I turned around. Yep, there was Elinor. Her frizz puffs popped sideways. She wore a bright orange collared shirt and tan corduroys, and her purple-framed eyeglasses were slightly crooked. The intensity in her face, her eyes, never seemed to match the way she looked or acted, except when she went manic on the monologues.

"Um, Madeline, I just wanted to tell you I'm really sorry for yesterday. I honestly didn't mean to eavesdrop. I just didn't know what to do. I mean, you guys came in, and before I could even make my presence known, you were crying, and so I just figured I should stay out of sight."

I glanced at her. "It's okay."

She smiled nervously at me. Then she just stood there.

Elinor was one of the first girls I met when I moved to Maine. Mac had put up a request for four farm interns on the school bulletin board, and she'd responded right away—to me. She came home with me that day and I went to her house once. We didn't click. But I was stuck sitting next to her in the few classes we had together, because of the E factor— Echols and Espinoza. She'd ramble on and on about things I didn't care about, like how different milking

31

procedures used to be at the turn of the last century. I mean, really.

I had nothing else to say, so I turned back to my locker and hoped she'd go away. I got one more glimpse of Thom's beyond-cute face, then grabbed my American history textbook and *To Kill a Mockingbird* and slid them into my metallic leather messenger bag. It was a gift from Caro—which meant she'd used it seven times and was sick of it.

I heard an intake of breath. Elinor was staring down the hall, and the crowd parted for the coming of Caro and Fergie. Elinor seemed frozen in place, then darted away.

Caro wrinkled her tiny nose in disgust as she approached me. "God, how do you stand having to talk to those people? I know you've got to do *some* campaigning for Most Popular, since the vote is only like six weeks away, but I would die if I had to talk to total losers like Frizz Puff."

"We *all* have to suffer for our crowns," Fergie added, bending down to rub the back of her foot. There was a blister visible under the black leather strap of her three-inch slingbacks. "Ow, ow, ow."

"That Frizz Puff chick is definitely going on the Not list this year," Caro said, pulling out her Black-Berry and making a notation. "Most in Need of an Extreme Makeover. Omigod, did you *see* her shoes? My aunt Daria used to wear those like thirty years ago. And those clown glasses? And come on, cords in May? It's like she's asking to be on the list. We'd be doing her a favor, really."

"She was on it last year," I reminded Caro. *Elinor Espinoza: Most in Need of an Extreme Makeover.*

As was my sister. *Sabrina Echols: Most in Need.*

Sabrina, a year older than I am, made the list every year, which was why I exempted myself from voting when I became eligible (end of ninth grade). Each class had its own little inner circle that created the Not list, so it wasn't like my friends put my sister on the list, but it was the principle.

"So? Did she get one? No. Until she does, she's top contender," Caro said, swiping Fergie's brush through her long blond hair. She hip-shook Fergie out of the mirror on the inside of my locker door.

"Hey!" Fergie complained, but took out a compact and lipstick and refreshed her sparkly pink-red lips.

"So you can't even imagine what it would feel like to be on that list?" I asked Caro.

She looked at me as if I were wearing a bad shirt. "No, I *can't*. Because I'd never be on it. No one *has* to be. People choose to look the way they do." She pointed her pale pink–tipped finger at Maya Blear, who was coming clearly uncomfortably down the hall, both emotionally and physically, her thighs audibly rubbing together. "She doesn't have to be two hundred pounds. There's something called a *diet*. She chooses to stuff her face with fries at lunch. Yesterday, I heard her ask for cheese on her fries! I eat carrot sticks for a reason. And what about this Fashion Don't?" she added, upping her chin at Jen Mercer. "No one forced her to buy that ugly weird shirt. She could have chosen a nicer one. I'm sure Wal-Mart has better choices than that."

Fergie snickered.

"I think it's more complicated than you're making it out to be," I told Caro as we headed down the hall to the cafeteria. The crowds in the hallway parted for us, as always, something that had taken me months to get used to when I first became part of their group. There was the usual gushing of "Hi!" and "I love your shoes!" and "I hope you can make the party!" I was the only one of us who smiled back. Caro and Fergie ignored everyone. And that was what made them even cooler.

"Yeah, we have choices," I told Caro. "But a lot of stuff gets in the way."

"Yeah, if you're a loser," Caro countered. "Sam sprained his ankle really bad and still finished the game last weekend—and won it for us. He made a *good* choice. It's all about choice."

The guy himself, his sandy-blond hair under a Red Sox cap, arrived at the cafeteria from the other direction at the same time we did. His best friends,

CJ—who everyone called Ceej—Tate, and Harry, were with him. The crowds parted for them, too. They were all good-looking and junior varsity captains of everything at Freeport Academy. Sam was actually *nice*. Ceej was okay, but Tate (Most Buff) and Harry (Most Hilarious) could be total jerks. Either Sam or Thom always won Most Beautiful and Most Popular. But they didn't seem to care about the labels, not the way my friends and I did.

Sam smiled. He had the warmest eyes, and they twinkled. His gaze lingered on me.

Caro positioned herself in front of me and linked arms with him. "Lead the way," she told him. If he led the way to a utility closet and stuck his hands up her top, then went back to the caf and ate a hamburger as though nothing had happened, that would be fine with her.

I had to admit—if I weren't crazy about Thom, who was still my boyfriend, three thousand miles away or not, I would be totally into Sam Fray. For all the reasons Caro liked him and more. He was different from most guys. He really was nice. Once, when Mac had sprained his wrist, Sam had stayed all day on a gorgeous Saturday just to help Mac and my mom usher the cows into pasture, when he could have joined all of us at the Coffee Connection before heading to the beach.

A few days ago, while my mother had gone on

and on during breakfast about the cost of protein to add to the cow feed this year, I'd thought about how wrong it was that a nice, gorgeous guy like Sam would never have a girlfriend at Freeport Academy while Caro wanted him.

That was power.

"So, have you heard from Thom?" Sam asked when he returned to our lunch table with his tray. His friends slid in beside him. As always, girls on one side, boys on the other. Caro liked it set up that way so that she could be on display. She wore a pale pink tank top that accentuated her breasts, her tan, and everything else about her perfect body.

"Like a hundred times since he left yesterday," I said, smiling. My phone vibrated. "And I think he just texted me."

I pulled out my phone. *You're probably at lunch. Say hi to everyone. I miss you. T*

"Thom says hi," I said, grinning and holding up the phone.

Fergie added exactly two tablespoons of dressing to her spinach salad. "You guys should still be on the ballot for Class Couple. I'm going to talk to the principal about that."

Caro tossed her long blond hair behind her

shoulder. "You totally should. I mean, they're *still* a couple. Right, Sam?"

Oh, so now we were still a couple? Or was that only for Sam's ears?

Sam glanced at me and shook salt on his fries. He offered a half-smile nod that seemed to say *I want to ask you out but I'm not sure if that's cool and that sucks.*

"James, Reid, come sit," Caro called out, waving over the two guys as they approached our table with their trays. They sometimes sat with us, but usually sat at the table behind ours with the sophomore cheerleaders because there was no room at our table. "Guys, you can squeeze in next to Madeline. She totally needs company now that Thom's gone."

Beyotch. I shot her a look, but her attention was on James and Reid.

I glanced up at James's cute face. He was very sought-after. Blond, the way Caro liked. But he didn't do anything for me. And the year before, I'd overheard him and another guy say some really mean stuff about a girl in my history class. And Reid was sort of vulgar, always telling farting jokes. No thanks.

James smiled, his gaze traveling down to my chest. Then he sat down on my left and hit my pinky with his tray. Smooth. He started going on and on about the past week's varsity baseball game, which his brother won for Freeport Academy. Caro shot me a look to listen. And *care*.

But I didn't. Not in the slightest. And when James's thigh brushed against mine, I moved just enough.

My cell vibrated again. A text from my mother.

Dad's invite here! XO Mom

This was almost as good as seeing Thom's name on the display. The invitation to my father's wedding had finally arrived. I'd been hounding my mother for a week about whether it had come. At first my father hadn't been sure if he and his fiancée were going to have a wedding or just do a quickie thing on the beach with a Buddhist minister and then jet off to Las Vegas for a honeymoon. But then he'd said his fiancée did want a wedding with family, which meant my sister and I were invited. Which meant I was definitely, officially going to California!

I texted Thom: *Start looking for a tux! Just got the invite to Dad's wedding! xoxo M*

"Oh, look, Madeline, there's your little friend," Caro whispered to me. "You can't tell me she's not the front-runner for Most in Need of an Extreme Makeover. Her hair alone nominates her." The whispering was for Sam's benefit, since Sam didn't participate in that kind of ragging on people. A few times, he'd gotten up and walked away, and Caro had caught on quickly.

I looked at Elinor Espinoza. She always walked with her head down, like she was ashamed to look anyone in the eye, so she often tripped—and just did. Something from Elinor's tray went flying and landed on the floor, and I could see that Elinor's face was bright red under all that hair. She was fighting back tears, I realized. She just stood there; then she turned and went running, sloshing around what was left on her tray.

Caro laughed. "Oh, she's totally taking Most in Need. Forget Makeover. She's beyond that." Out came the BlackBerry.

Mean. Mean. Mean. Another reason I couldn't wait for my dad's wedding was that I'd get away from Freeport, away from Maine, away from Caro.

I glanced up and caught Sam looking at me. Caro, spearing spinach leaves, had that slightly tight expression she got when she was about to rag on something—or someone. She didn't, though; she just stabbed a cherry tomato and bit into it. Slowly.

Forget it, I thought. *You are going to California in three and a half weeks! And maybe,* I let myself think, *maybe you're not coming back.*

My cell vibrated with another text from Thom. *Wish you were here. XXXX T*

I wished I were there too. And maybe I *could* be there.

I could live with my dad.

Twenty minutes from Thom's new house. And Thom was going to a private school that I could enroll in.

I'd been thinking about it for the past two weeks. At first, it had just been a little daydream, a fantasy. But the more I thought about being without Thom, and the weirder things between me and Caro grew, the more moving in with my dad and his new wife-to-be sounded . . . perfect.

Right. Leave my mom and sister. Leave Mac, my stepdad, who was more a father to me than my own father.

Leave Caro and Fergie and Annie and Selena. Lately? In a heartbeat.

Chapter 4

I hadn't told anyone about my big plan, the one I couldn't stop thinking about. The one that felt more right by the minute.

How could I? *Um, Mom, when you're done with the afternoon milking, I need to let you know I'm thinking of moving in with Dad. Permanently.*

I loved my mom, and Mac was a really nice guy. He was one of those perfect stepfathers, the kind who never tried to tell you what to do, but always had really good advice. Plus he was nuts about my mom, and my mom was kind of nuts, a cross between a hippie and a farm girl. She was really into the earth and recycling and being green. Mac was the same. I had seen him cry at least ten times over losing a calf or selling some livestock. They both got really attached to the animals.

But I wasn't meant for farm life. I hated everything about it, from the sight of tractors to the smell of poop to the mind-numbing roosters crowing at daybreak.

I *belonged* in California. I knew that for a fact. And if I lived with my dad, we could get back how things used to be between us. When he and my mom were still married, we were really close. Not that he was around much, which was one of the reasons my parents divorced. But when he was, he'd make these huge messy meals for me and Sabrina, like sloppy joes and french fries and banana splits, and when Sabrina would go off to study, I'd stay and talk to my dad about stuff, like feeling invisible, and not understanding algebra, and being incredibly annoyed by Sabrina. He'd listen and give funny advice and make me feel heard. But ever since he'd moved to California and found Tiffany, his soon-to-be third wife, it was like he focused on her and forgot about me and Sabrina (not that he and Sabrina were ever very close).

With my mom and Mac, it was different. They listened—and I totally gave them credit for it—but they didn't understand me at all. After I came home from visiting my aunt in Rome, I heard them talking in their bedroom late at night, and my mom was saying something like "I think it's so cute that Madeline is such a sophisticate. She's really her own person and marches to her own drummer." In other words, I was normal.

I didn't really fit into my family. *They* were the weirdos, with their thigh-high forest green rubber boots and dinner-length discussions about how cows had four stomachs. To them, *I* was the freak in the three-inch-high sandals who preferred to read *Lucky* magazine instead of *Livestock Daily*.

My dad? Totally normal. A California architect with a BMW, an iPhone, and a gym membership. Living with him, enrolling in Thom's school, living the life I wanted seemed so doable. Except for the part about my mom and Mac and even Sabrina being three thousand miles away.

I wished I could talk to my sister about this, but I couldn't. Sabrina would call me a traitor. *Stop idolizing Dad,* she always snapped at me. *Look where it got Mom and Deirdre.* Deirdre was his second wife, and though the word "homewrecker" was thrown around a lot right after my dad moved into her condo when we lived in the suburbs of New York City, she was really nice. It had been mostly Sabrina who'd used the word "homewrecker."

When I got home from school, Sabrina was sitting at the kitchen table, eating a fish taco and reading a book on animal husbandry. You'd think living on the farm would be enough, but no, Sabrina liked to read up on the care and feeding of livestock in her nonworking hours. She was sporting her trade-mark look: a bandana around her head (and not in a retro way), baggy overalls (she had them in four different washes), and brown clogs. No makeup. She didn't even use gel or mousse in her short hair. She just got out of the shower and put on the farmer outfit, and she was ready. She could be cute, if she tried. But she honestly didn't seem to care.

The way she dressed wasn't the main reason she made the Not list every year; it was that combined with the handmade signs she liked to wear around her neck or write on her T-shirts with marker, such as *Cows are people too*. There were a lot of things wrong with that, but the biggest one was that cows weren't people.

She also had a nervous habit of saying weird things when she was uncomfortable. If a popular girl said, "Excuse me," because, say, Sabrina was blocking the path to the water fountain, Sabrina would get all flustered and blurt out something like "Did you know that cows have four stomachs?"

So people looked at her like she was a total weirdo, then walked away. Except for the people just like her, and believe it or not, there were a few. Sabrina had a best friend and two other girls she hung around with.

A dollop of salsa landed on the page of her book, but she didn't seem to notice, because she was staring out the bay window at the bare-chested hotness of Sam. Crushes on cute guys were definitely something that all girls had in common. But then I saw she wasn't staring at Sam, but at Joe, a junior farm intern who was so gawky it was a wonder the hay bale he was carrying didn't send him flying over backward. I'd never heard Joe speak, but then again, I didn't spend much time on the farm.

Like Sabrina, Sam wanted to be a vet. For horses and cows and goats, not house pets. This was why he preferred to rake manure and lead the cows out to pasture in his free time. Anyone at the high school could earn three science credits by working at my parents' small dairy farm in an internship program for an entire school year, including the dead of winter, which in Maine was pretty brutal. My mom and Mac had four interns this year—in addition to two full-time farmhands. They mostly cleaned up cow poop (which meant raking it into the gutters in front of the cow pens), made sure the cows and calves had fresh water, fed the calves from their bottles, put out the feed for the cows, and did some light grooming and cleaning. Sam was the only hot intern. The rest looked like . . . well, like farmers.

"Where is it?" I asked Sabrina, dumping my messenger bag on a chair.

"Where's what?" she asked, taking a bite of her taco.

I rolled my eyes. "The invitation!"

She shrugged. "Don't know, don't care."

Grr! She infuriated me. Could we be any more different? *Don't care in the slightest* was her response to making the Not list again last year. *Like I care what some shallow, vapid airheads in fancy clothes think of me. Why* would *I?*

Sometimes I thought her attitude was a good thing, mostly because, like my aunt Darcy said, people were who they were and should be celebrated for their uniqueness, not ridiculed. Sabrina, according to Aunt Darcy, was her own person and could one day be president. I wasn't sure about that. Maybe president of the Future Farmers of America Club.

I glanced around the kitchen, in the usual spots that our mother left things for us, like notes and ten-dollar bills, but I didn't see anything resembling a fancy envelope.

"Well, do you know where Mom is?" I asked.

"In the calves' barn."

I exchanged my silver sandals—you couldn't *not* step in something gross at the farm, especially in the barns—for my Crocs and headed out to the calves' barn. It was around fifty feet from the house. It wasn't one of those old-fashioned red barns like in children's picture books. It was just an ugly weathered shingled structure, somewhere between brown and gray, with corrals and pens, lots of hay, and rakes. You had to hold your nose when you entered. Well, I did.

I didn't see my mother, but I did see Elinor at the far end. She was sitting on an upside-down metal bucket and feeding a calf, but she was also staring at Sam as he raked out a stall. She didn't seem to notice that Weasley was sucking on air, and even I knew that that wasn't good for a calf.

I heard Sam say to her, "Did you know the bottle's empty? Boy, Weasley sucks fast."

Instead of answering him, Elinor froze; she looked like she had in Latin 1 the day before when she'd stood up to present her Greek myth. She'd had to sit back down and try again later. Elinor dropped the bottle and ran past me toward the house, presumably to ask Mac for more milk, but I knew she was probably standing outside the barn, breaking into hives.

"Oh, Madeline, there you are," my mother said, coming around the side of the barn. She tightened the ponytail holder on her long braid, then pulled a large envelope from the sling she always wore across her chest.

Yes! California, here I come!

"Someone's excited," my mom said with a smile,

47

but then one of the farmhands called her for help; she was having trouble moving a cow. "Show me later," she called over her shoulder as she hurried off.

In the middle of the stinky barn, two ever-present giant ducks waddled past me as I tore open the envelope. There was no point in opening it with Sabrina, since she hated our dad's guts at the moment. It had been a long moment—since he'd moved to California three years earlier.

I pulled out the invitation, a cream-colored card with fancy calligraphy.

Tiffany Alison Bluthwell and Timothy Lee Echols cordially invite you to share in the celebration of their wedding. . . .

I flipped through the layers of see-through tissue paper. But there were only two little cards, one with directions to the wedding and one a reply card. No note about having booked the airline tickets?

I rushed inside. "Look, the invitation to Dad's wedding," I said to Sabrina. "I guess he'll book our plane tickets when we know exactly when we want to leave and return, right?"

She glanced at the address on the outer envelope. "Sabrina and Madeline Echols? He couldn't even send us each our own invitation," she grumbled over a mouthful of food. She shook her head. "Nice, Dad. So fatherly."

"We live in the *same* house, Sabrina," I pointed out. She was such a downer. "We're going to L.A.! Sabrina, we'll see A-list celebrities in line at Starbucks!" *And Thom,* I added to myself.

"No we won't," she said. "Because *we're* not going. I wouldn't go if he *sent* us tickets, which I assume he won't. And *you* won't go because you can't afford a ticket from Maine to L.A. And you're *not* asking Mom and Mac. They can't afford it either. So don't be a total brat and ask, Maddie."

I hated, hated, hated being called Maddie. And Sabrina knew it. I was Maddie before freshman year, before my European transformation. Maddie was a different girl.

I searched the envelope again for a personal note from our dad saying that he'd book e-tickets, that we could, of course, stay in their gorgeous condo (which I got a glimpse of in their last Christmas card photo, with my dad and Tiffany and her little white dog in front of a white Christmas tree), which wasn't on the beach, but close. But there was nothing. "I'm sending this back with a 'Miss Madeline Echols *will* attend.'"

"I'd change my outfit if I were you," Sabrina said, eyeing my white capris. "You'll be working the farm every minute until the wedding. Not that you'll earn enough to pay your way. Just forget it. He doesn't even care if we come, Madeline."

"I think he does," I said, sounding more confident than I felt.

And I was confident about something else, too: I *was* going to that wedding.

"I wish I could, sweetie," my father said on the phone. It was four o'clock in Maine but one o'clock in California. I imagined him at his desk, eating lunch. My dad built food courts in airports. He used to build cafeterias in schools. When I was the new kid in middle school and sitting alone pretty much all the time for lunch, I would imagine that he'd made the cafeteria, and I'd feel comforted. "But every cent is going to pay for the wedding. I mean, the cake alone cost a fortune—it has, like, ten layers or something. You know I'd love for you and Sabrina to come, Mads, but I just can't swing the fare. A one-way ticket is over three hundred, honey. I checked. It's just going to be a small ceremony, anyway. You can see it all on video."

How personal.

I wouldn't tell Sabrina this. It would only fuel her hatred.

"But I haven't even met Tiffany," I reminded him, dropping onto the edge of my bed. "You're marrying someone I haven't even met. And you've been together over a year." I'd been so focused on

50

going to California to be with Thom that I hadn't even realized until now how much I wanted to go for my dad, to spend some time with him on his turf, to feel a part of his life. To get back what we'd had before the divorce.

"I know, hon," he said. "Once we're back from the honeymoon, maybe we can plan a trip to Maine. Tiff's never been to Maine. She wasn't even sure if Maine was part of Canada or the U.S. Isn't that amazing?"

Amazingly stupid. I'd never been to California and I knew it wasn't part of Mexico.

My father would marry Tiffany, who I'd never met, and she would never want to come to Maine, because she already lived on a gorgeous coast. I got the point of traveling from Maine to California: for L.A., Hollywood, movie stars, palm trees. But in Maine, there was only good lobster. And according to my father, Tiff was not only a vegetarian, but a vegan, which meant she didn't eat anything that came from a cow or a chicken or a goat, like milk or cheese or eggs. I could forget her ever setting foot on a dairy farm.

I could also forget about moving to California. I could forget about Thom.

We talked for a few minutes and then he had to go. I lay down and covered my face with a pillow, then bolted up. *No way.* My aunt Darcy always said that when life handed you a box of chocolates with the gross pink cream stuff inside that you hated, you could either throw out the whole box and be depressed or you could bite around the pink cream and be in chocolate heaven. According to Aunt Darcy, there was a way around *every* hurdle.

I sat down at my desk and turned on my laptop. A quick check of e-mail—two short but very sweet messages from Thom. He'd gotten lost on the way to Western civ, but he'd already been befriended by some of the popular people.

I immediately thought of a beautiful blonde in a pink bikini.

I clicked onto Google and typed *cheap airline tickets* into the search box. Apparently the cheapest airline ticket from Portland, Maine, to Los Angeles, California, on June fifth *was* $332 one way. Just like my dad had said.

At least he had looked into it. That was something.

And at least I only needed a one-way ticket. Well, to get there. I was *pretty* sure my father would be happy to have me move in with him and Tiffany. It wasn't like I was a little kid who needed their attention. I could take care of myself. I wouldn't be in the way of their newlywed whatever. I'd be out with Thom all the time, anyway.

And if my dad wasn't into the idea of having me

move in, he'd have to pay for a return ticket to get rid of me, wouldn't he?

But how was I going to come up with $332? And as we got closer to the travel date, the fare would likely go up. I'd need to come up with $400 just to be safe. But how?

I wasn't sixteen yet, not until October, so I couldn't even vow to pay my parents back with the money from the summer job I wouldn't be able to get.

I flopped back onto my bed with my favorite photo of me and Thom, the one taken the previous winter break in his backyard. It was just us and the snowman we'd built; I was on one side and Thom was on the other and we were hugging each other through it, snow all over us. Thom looked happy. And so did I.

There was no snow in California. No snow to re-mind Thom of that day.

Channel Aunt Darcy, I told myself, eyes closed, photo clutched against my chest. My amazing aunt's face floated into my mind, her chic swingy bob, her red lipstick that no one else could pull off, her in-credible sense of style. What would Aunt Darcy do?

She would think of something. And so would I.

Chapter 5

I flipped to a blank page in my English notebook and wrote *WAYS TO EARN LOTS OF MONEY FAST* across the top. Ten minutes later, I still had nothing. Babysitting at the going rate of eight dollars an hour would get me as far as New Hampshire, maybe. Working at the farm every day after school and on weekends at the non-intern rate of five bucks an hour would get me—

"Hello? Madeline? It's me, Elinor. Espinoza?" This was followed by three quick knocks on my closed bedroom door.

Elinor Espinoza? Why? And why was she *everywhere?* This time I had no intimidating friends to send her running away.

There was another series of knocks. "Madeline?"

Sigh. I closed my notebook and threw it aside, then got up and opened the door. Elinor, clutching a red backpack with raccoons all over it and *EE* monogrammed in purple thread, stood in the doorway.

"There's something else I've been wanting to talk to you about. I mean, besides this morning."

I waited, watching the way one of the frizz puffs bounced with her every breath.

"Can I come in?"

I held the door open and she stepped in and glanced nervously around, like she expected Caro or Fergie to pop out and grab her.

"It's about the list. The Not list."

"Okay," I said, waiting. Actually, I was about to explode. *Get to the* point.

She took a deep breath. "I have exactly one hundred dollars in here," she said, pulling wads of cash from the backpack. "Is that enough?"

"Enough for what?" I asked.

She took another deep breath, and then her words came out in a rush. "To keep me off the Not list. Most Nerdy. Most in Need of an Extreme Makeover. Most in Need. Most Not Cool. You know."

"To keep you off the list? What are you talking about?"

"Fine, I'll just say it. I'll pay you to keep me off that list. So is a hundred enough?" she asked, staring at me. Her lower lip started to tremble.

I couldn't believe she was bribing me. "Elinor,

honestly, I have nothing to do with the list. I'm not lying."

"Well, you have influence with your friends, I'm sure."

I dead-eyed her. "So you want to pay me a hundred bucks to tell my friends not to put you on the list."

"Yes," she said. "That's exactly what I want."

If a hundred bucks would get me to California, I would almost consider doing it. But I'd need an entire backpack full of those crumpled ones and fives that she'd clearly taken out of her piggy bank that morning.

"Elinor, if you want off the list so badly, why not just take your hundred dollars and get a makeover? Just go to the mall." I stared at the horizontal frizz puff. "Start with a hair salon. A lot of them even offer brow waxing, too. Then go to one of the makeup counters in a department store. You don't even have to buy anything. Oh, and you could get new glasses, too. And new clothes at the outlets in Freeport. A whole new look."

"Riiiight," she said slowly. "So all it takes is a new hairstyle and a few new outfits and suddenly I'm in?"

Well, not *in* so much as not *on* the Not list. Some girls faded into the woodwork and were sort of invisible, which meant they never appeared on the

Not list. The ones who stood out for being notice-ably weird were the ones who made the list. Like Elinor. And Sabrina.

"That's how I did it," I reminded her.

She stared at me for a moment, then shook her head. "No, Madeline. That's *not* how you did it. You didn't just change your hair and get expensive jeans and cool shoes. You changed *yourself*. Big difference."

Actually, I hadn't. I had always been *me*. I'd just changed the outside to match the inside, which was what my aunt Darcy had taught me how to do that summer I visited her in Rome.

The moment Aunt Darcy's little car had zoomed into the city, I had been transfixed. And when she took me to an outdoor café, where she introduced me to real cappuccinos, I couldn't take my eyes off a table of Italian girls nearby. The way they were dressed. The way they wore their hair. They way they laughed and enjoyed themselves. And when a group of boys came over, I studied the way the girls flirted yet remained mysterious. In control. Unat-tainable.

And I told my aunt Darcy I was meant to be an Italian girl. She was delighted, and all day we people-watched and then she took me shopping in boutiques, where the saleswomen taught me how to put together an interesting outfit that was chic and smart. I watched Italian girls without having any idea what they were saying in their beautiful language. I didn't need to know. I just needed to study them. By the end of the month, in my new clothes with European flair, and with long layers cut into my formerly blah straight brown hair that now shone and swung with the right hair products, and with the new, confident way I spoke to waiters and hotel staff and Aunt Darcy's friends, I was an Italian girl. Add to that the transformation my body underwent that summer—finally, from lanky and flat-chested to slightly curvy with an almost–B cup (pure biology)—and I was unrecognizable when I went home to Maine.

My mother and Mac had been quite amused when they'd picked the new me up from the jetport. They were big believers in becoming the you-est you, and if being a glamour queen like Aunt Darcy was the me-est me, so be it. They wanted only people who loved the farm to work the farm. People who loved the herd, loved the ducks and hens and chickens, loved the smell of wet hay, loved even the machinery. They thought the animals, and the very minerals in the land, *knew*. So I was exempt from farm duty.

"Anyway, I thought you said you just want off the list, Elinor. That's a lot easier than becoming a Most. You just have to not stand out so much."

She stepped inside and closed the door. "So help me. Fix me. Tell me *how*."

How could I tell her to change every single thing about herself and sound like a decent human being? Everything, from the frizz puffs to the socks she wore with her granny sandals to what she talked about, was just *wrong*.

I let out a deep breath. "Elinor, I'm sorry, but I'm just not the right per—"

"So you won't take the money?"

"No, I won't take the money."

She glared at me, looking like she was about to cry. "God, it must be nice to live such a charmed life that you can turn down a hundred bucks to do something so simple and easy, something that would make such a big difference in someone's life. Thanks a lot."

What did she know? "Oh, yes, Elinor, my charmed life. I can't even get to my own father's wedding because a ticket costs over three hundred bucks. Which means I can't ask him if I can live with him. Which means I can't—"

What was I doing? Why was I telling Elinor Espinoza my life story? I shut up fast.

"You're going to ask your dad if you can live with him? Do you think he'll say yes?"

I shrugged. "Of course. He's my dad, right?"

She bit her lip and nodded. "And you'd just

59

leave your friends? Your great life here? Just like that?"

"Sometimes a change is just what a person needs," I said.

"Yeah," she said. "I know."

I didn't comment. She glanced around. "You changed your room since I was here last. I like it."

She'd been "here last" three years before, when she'd first started interning. When we'd moved here, I was obsessed with having a giant rainbow painted on the big wall, lots of pictures of unicorns, and a pink bed with white furniture. By the time I returned from Rome, my room seemed so babyish. Now it was painted a pale blue, and there were a Japanese rock garden and bamboo. It was all very Zen and supposed to make me think calm thoughts.

The Zen room wasn't helping at the moment.

"Madeline? You up here?" my mother called as she came up the stairs, gave a quick knock on the door, and opened it. "Oh, Elinor, hello. I'll just come back later."

Elinor picked up her backpack. "That's okay, Mrs. Sklar." Sklar was Mac's last name. Elinor hurried out of my room, not bothering to say goodbye.

She was so weird. Good thing she kept her hundred bucks. Because there was nothing I could do for her.

• • •

I called Thom. No answer. I left a message.

An hour later, I tried again. No answer.

Of course I was panicking. Picturing him with the pink bikini chick.

But then, a half hour later, my cell rang and I jumped for it. *Thom!*

"Hey," he said, and for a moment it felt as if he still lived just a few blocks away. As if nothing had changed.

"Hey," I said back. "I'm trying to work out the details of when I'll be flying in for the wedding. Probably June fifth, the day before."

"Cool," he said. "I've really missed you."

At least he said he missed me. But there was something sort of . . . different about his voice. Or maybe I was being paranoid.

Just ask him. Just say Thom, we're okay, right? We're still a couple? You're not dating a girl in a pink bikini? You still love me?

"Thom, I—"

There were some muffled sounds in the background. "Hey, Mad, the rest of the team is here. I gotta go," Thom said, sounding rushed. "See ya."

"I love you," I said into the nothingness, and I imagined him saying it back.

I had to get to California.

Chapter 6

I was putting the finishing touches on my essay for English—about how Scout felt about her father in *To Kill a Mockingbird*—when the bell rang. Not a school bell, but our early-morning farm bell. Time for the interns to put down their buckets and brushes and rakes and head to the bunkhouse, which had four small private bathrooms with showers and sinks and everything an intern might need to spruce up for school. Once a week in the spring and summer, the interns showed up to work an hour and a half before school. The bell meant there was twenty minutes until the bus stopped at the end of the long driveway.

I rarely took the bus to school. Usually, Caro's live-in housekeeper picked up me and Fergie every morning and drove us home every afternoon. A live-in housekeeper—now *that* made for a charmed life.

I'd been working on my essay for three days

and had almost forgotten it was due that day. It was a surprisingly good book about this girl named Scout (which I thought was the coolest name) whose dad was a lawyer defending someone for a crime he didn't commit but everyone in town blamed him for. It was about standing up for what you believed, doing what was right, even when everyone was against you. My dad would do what was right—I was pretty sure, anyway. But wasn't what was right making sure his daughters could attend his wedding? Even if it was his third?

"Hello? Madeline? It's Elinor. And Avery. Hello?" I heard whispering from the other side of my closed bedroom door. Then there was a knock.

Elinor and Avery? Who was Avery?

"Come in," I called out, saving my essay.

Elinor opened the door. Beside her was a girl I'd seen a couple of times on the farm. One of the interns? I hit print and waited for someone to start speaking. They crowded in, Elinor slightly in front.

"This is Avery Kennar," Elinor said. "She just started interning here last week."

"You actually do schoolwork?" Avery asked me, craning her neck to peer at my printer.

I collected the papers and stapled them, then slipped the report into my English notebook and slid that into my messenger bag. "Of course. What did you think?"

"I don't know," she said. "That maybe you had people do it for you. I saw that in a movie once. This girl paid five different really smart kids to do her homework and write her papers." Her hand flew to her mouth. "Not that you aren't smart. That's not what I meant."

"Yes, I actually do my homework and write my own papers," I said. *Weirdo.*

Elinor was just standing there staring at me. Her hair was even poufier than it had been the day before, probably because it was one of those overcast, humid days when it felt a lot hotter than it really was. She wore plaid Bermuda shorts and a navy blue T-shirt—with, for some reason, a shiny dark gray vest and scuffed white sneakers with weird sporty swirls on them. There were dark red pompoms peeking out of the sneakers.

Elinor cleared her throat. "We have a proposition for you, Madeline. You said you needed over three hundred dollars. Between the two of us, we have three hundred and fifty dollars. We want to pay you to help us change our images."

The girl did not give up! Were they seriously going to pay me three hundred and fifty bucks to tell Fergie and Caro to take their names out of the running? That was crazy. "I told you I can't—"

"No," Elinor interrupted, adjusting her purple plastic glasses on her nose. "This isn't a bribe. We want you to teach us, like a class, how to get less *un*popular. Show us how to change. We want you to change us from the inside out."

"The inside out?" I repeated. "How am I supposed to do that?"

"The same way *you* did it," Elinor said. "You learned the secrets. Now teach us."

"Um, if I can say something?" Avery cut in. "Madeline clearly started out with an advantage: she's *very* pretty. I'm not exactly ever going to win Most Beautiful." But she wasn't ugly. Or even plain. She was actually almost cute. She had straight shoulder-length brown hair and wore khaki capris and a pink tank top and perfectly fine sandals.

"But she could show you how to look as good as you *can*," Elinor said. "That's what Madeline knows; that's what she's always understood. And she can teach us much, much more," she went on. "As I talked about while we were washing the milking tubes, getting off the list takes more than just a new look."

What had Elinor promised this Avery chick? "I'm *not* a teacher," I said, turning a glare on Elinor. "And I'm not running a Learning Annex class."

"Please?" Elinor said, folding her hands together in front of her. "I really, really need this. I really need to change. God, I just want to be . . . *normal*."

I looked at their hopeful faces as they waited for

me to say yes. I stared at Avery. She didn't need much help. A little makeup, some trendier clothes. She had the basics.

"I just moved here from Massachusetts and it's like I'm totally invisible," Avery said. "I look like everyone else, just like I did in my last school, and I wasn't exactly Miss Popularity there, either. I want to stand out. And I have no idea how. I've tried talking to people, but they ignore me. I overheard Sam Fray say he was interning at a dairy farm, so I signed up for it too. I figured the proximity to a popular guy would help. Like maybe I could get to be friends with him and then he'd sort of introduce me to his friends."

"Has it worked?" I asked her.

She shook her head. "He wears an iPod most of the time and never hears me when I say hi. And he seems really into the work."

"Sam is very out of our league," Elinor said. "And anyway, standing out can be dangerous, Avery. That's the reason I always make the Not list in the first place."

"Well, I don't want to look *worse*," Avery said. "I want to look *better*. I want to look more than better—I want to look like you, Madeline, and your friends." Elinor stared at her with pride, at this girl who dared to dream big. "I just don't know *how*. Even when I go shopping and try stuff on that I see you and your friends wearing, I just look . . . stupid. Like I'm trying too hard or something. Does that make sense?"

"Yeah, I understand what you mean." I did, because I used to *be* Avery.

"So?" Elinor said to me. "Three hundred and fifty bucks to teach us how to be more . . . normal before the Not list comes out."

"This is crazy," I said. "In what, four, five weeks' time, I'm supposed to turn you both into totally different people?"

They nodded.

"Different enough to not make the Not list," Elinor said. "That's what I want. And Avery wants to look better enough to possibly make the Most list! Yay, A!" she added. "Omigod, that rhymes!"

Omigod was right. Was she really this corny? If she said something like that around Caro and Fergie, they'd torment her with it forever.

"Three hundred and fifty dollars," Elinor repeated, knowing that would cover what I needed. "I'm paying more, since I need the most help and I'm planning on passing what I learn to my sister. She's in middle school, but it's never too early."

I pictured my dad marrying a woman I'd never met. I pictured Thom and the blond girl in a bikini in math class. He was pulling the·strings to her top. She was giggling.

Maybe some lessons in how to be popular—how not to be a total dork, really—wouldn't be such a big deal. A few hours of my life here and there for three hundred and fifty bucks. For California.

"We can give you half the money right now and the other half in two weeks," Elinor said. "That's when I'll have the last hundred from babysitting the Cotter twins. They're four."

I took a very deep breath. *California. California. California.* Half the money in my possession now, to make it feel real. And the other half in two weeks.

"Okay. I'll do it," I told them. "I'll try to change your image. But I can't guarantee anything." *I'm a high school sophomore—not a miracle worker.*

Elinor started jumping up and down and clapping. The almost cute girl took a deep breath.

"Elinor, lesson number one," I said. "Don't jump."

The interns, excluding Sam, who rode his bike to the farm and to school most days, were waiting in their cluster by the Blueberry Ledge Farm sign at the main road. I sat on a huge rock—on my English notebook—across the dirt driveway, waiting for Mandy, Caro's housekeeper, to pull up. Caro lived in an amazing house a mile away on the Atlantic

Ocean. The first time Caro had invited me over, I'd thought her house was one of those fancy bed-and-breakfasts. That was how big it was, how grand. Mandy had been with the Alexander family forever, since Caro and her older brother (he was in college already) were babies, so Caro treated her with a degree of respect.

Elinor whispered something to Joe, the other guy intern, and he looked over at me. Now *there* was someone who could use a little fashion advice. He wore a T-shirt tucked into blue shorts. All that was missing were kneesocks.

"Could I ask you something?" he said to me.

Oh God. I nodded.

"I'm sort of interested in going in on this thing that Elinor and Avery are doing. But, I'm a guy, you know? It's not like you can give me advice on makeup or whatever."

"She can help you be more like her boyfriend and his friends," Avery said. "How to dress, how to act, what to say."

Wait a minute. Two girls, fine. Now there was a guy in the mix?

"So you can really teach me how to talk to people?" Joe asked me. "I never know what to say, so I never say anything, and then when I get home, I suddenly think of what I should have said."

And yet that was quite a mouthful.

"With Joe in, your fee can be an even four hundred," Elinor said. "If that helps."

It helped.

"So do you think you could help me?" he asked. "Be less a total dork? I'm totally aware I am a dork, mostly because I get called a dork loser ten times a day."

That had to suck. Worse than being completely ignored and invisible was being tortured.

"I could try," I said.

Joe shrugged. "Okay, I'm in."

Elinor did her little clapping jump again. Avery just eyed me.

Great. Just great. Now there were three.

When Mandy's car pulled up, the interns backed away, as they always did, as if they were afraid Caro would wave her magic wand at them and turn them into trolls or something. Mandy's car was small, a Honda Civic, so it wasn't like I could invite the interns to ride with us. As if Caro would let them in the car, anyway.

"God, Madeline," Caro said as we pulled onto the main road. "Remember when you used to be friends with that weirdo Frizz Puff girl?" She slicked on some lip gloss. "It's almost amazing, really, that you went from hanging out with *that* to hanging out with us."

Fergie laughed next to me. "Your life could have been so different, Madeline."

As Fergie searched through her purse for something, I could feel Caro's eyes on me. I wouldn't look at her, wouldn't give her the satisfaction of knowing she'd reminded me of where I'd come from. And if there had been a threat in there somewhere, that she could kick me to the curb anytime, I really didn't want to acknowledge it. Or think about it.

I hadn't been friends with Elinor. She'd just talked my ear off in classes and trailed after me, talking away. We hadn't been friends.

But now I'd be hanging out with Nots a few times a week for the "class."

I'd need to make it clear to my friends that I *wasn't* hanging out with them.

"So you will never believe what the interns— excluding Sam, of course—at my parents' farm are paying me to do for them," I began, then launched into the whole story. About my dad's wedding, the cost of airfare, how I was dying to go so I could also spend time with Thom.

I didn't mention my plan to ask my dad if I could live with him. I didn't think voluntarily moving three thousand miles away from your best friends would go over well. Then again, Caro probably wouldn't mind. If she'd had the money herself, she would probably have given it to me just to separate me from Sam. Caro's family was rich, but they were tightwad rich. A lot of Caro's amazing clothes and shoes and handbags were hand-me-downs from her mother, a fashionista size four. Caro rarely bought anything new, but then again, she didn't have to.

Caro wouldn't give me the money to go chasing after Thom. She wanted me to hook up with someone at Freeport Academy, someone who'd take me off the available list.

"So what do you think I should teach them?" I asked. How was I supposed to even teach them anything? Did I just tell them each how to look better? What to say when a guy said, "See you in school"?

They were both staring at me as though I'd sprouted another head, the crazy head that had made me agree to such a thing.

"Please tell me you're kidding about doing this," Caro said as Mandy pulled into the Freeport Academy parking lot. "You're going to help a bunch of freaky loser farm interns so that maybe they'll be normal enough not to make the Not list."

I glanced at Mandy to see if she'd give Caro a look for being so mean, but she didn't. She never did.

"Right," Fergie answered for me. "That's how I heard it."

"And does that make any sense to you?" Caro asked.

"Oddly, yes," Fergie said. "Madeline is Most Popular. She's teaching them how to be more like her."

"Right. Because all it takes is some advice on clothes and makeup and conversation to be like us," Caro said. "They're throwing away their money."

Maybe not. I had some cute clothes of my own and some hand-me-downs from Caro and Fergie. (Selena wasn't a great dresser, and Annie was a bit hopeless in the style department and tended to go sporty.) I had a pair of Sevens that my aunt Darcy had bought me in Rome and some very nice tops and shoes. Why couldn't I just put Elinor in the outfit I was wearing now? Cute flippy skirt. White T-shirt, interesting necklace. Great sandals. She could borrow some of my stuff the way I borrowed a lot of Caro's and Fergie's clothes.

I shrugged. "If Elinor straightened her hair or cut it and lost the headband and maybe got new glasses and new clothes and stood straight—"

"Madeline, you are way too nice," Caro broke in. "Yeah, she could change her clothes and lose the stupid glasses. But what about her entire personality?" She added, laughing, "Mosts are *born,* darling. Not *made.*"

"I totally agree," Fergie said. "Take you, for example, Madeline. You were a Most in boring clothes and blah hair before you went to Rome. But you were *always* a Most. I mean, don't be so *shallow*. Being a Most is more than how you look on the outside; it's the kind of person you are on the *in-side*. And everyone knows that's what really counts. Like, if you lost everything in a flood or something and had to fashion a top and pants out of a garbage bag, you'd still be a Most inside. Because you'd still be *you*. You'd still *rule*."

Wow. That was . . . so sideways.

And of course Caro was beaming at Fergie.

The Nots were in trouble.

Chapter 7

In history class, as Mr. Fortunata droned on about President Kennedy and Cuba, I tried to figure out how exactly I was going to impart my mighty wisdom to the interns. The Not list was always decided a few days before the Most list came out, which was on the Monday before school ended. That gave me almost five weeks to spin straw into gold.

Hmmm. I figured I could go through my stack of magazines and flag pictures of trendy clothes. And hairstyles. And maybe I could give the interns a list of TV shows to watch that might help them socially. I could give them a cheat sheet of things I picked up when I was in Italy.

But I couldn't overwhelm them. I'd have to start small. For Elinor, the hair. Just doing something about the horizontal frizz puffs would make a big difference. For Joe, we'd untuck the shirt. And Avery . . . she would be tricky, because nothing was glaringly wrong. I glanced around the class, trying to get ideas.

And there she was. Watching me.

Avery was in this class? I'd never noticed.

I shot her a quick smile, and she smiled back. Did she always surprise people like that? Well, no wonder she had no friends. We'd start with mentioning things like *I'm in your history class*.

I glanced back and she was still staring at me.

So was Sam. He sat one row behind, diagonally across. I smiled, and he smiled that dazzling smile of his, then glanced down at his textbook.

He *did* like me. There was no denying it.

And there was no denying that it gave me a secret thrill. Not because he found me prettier than Caro. But because . . . I wasn't sure exactly. I didn't like Sam that way. Well, maybe a teeny, tiny bit if I was very honest.

The bell rang, and Avery was out like a shot. She was making this easy. *Lesson number two, Avery: Say hi to the popular person you actually know instead of fleeing the room.* That was how you made friends and showed people you were on chatting terms with the popular crowd.

I closed my notebook, full of useless notes about transforming the interns, slid it into my messenger bag, and checked my cell for a text from Thom.

Hey, thinking about you. Wish you were here. I keep saying that. XXT. I grinned. His e-mails and texts and calls were getting fewer, but quick kisses were still kisses. I texted back a *Ditto* and some kisses of my own.

Soon I would be there. And maybe forever.

"Hey," Sam called after me. "You forgot your textbook." He handed it to me. "Lost in thought?" His gaze lingered on my face.

Again a funny feeling—but in a *good* weird way—attacked my stomach. I nodded. "Seems to be all the time lately."

"Thom, right?" he asked as we headed down the hall.

"Thom and a lot of stuff, actually." Like my father, who was getting married to a woman I'd never met. The weird vibe from Caro. And the bizarre way I was going to earn the money to fix the first two things.

"Well, you know, Madeline, if you ever need to talk . . ."

He really was good-looking. No wonder so many girls were crazy in lust with him. I'd always known he was amazingly cute, but just then, the way he was focused on me, those warm brown eyes on me . . . for just a moment, I found myself unable to look away.

No. Look away, Madeline. And focus.

"Um, Sam, actually, I could use your advice about something. If you were going to help someone change his image, how would you do it? I mean, how would you go about it? Where would you start?"

"I guess I'd start with asking what he wanted to change."

Good idea. I could ask the interns what they wanted to change most, what they really wanted to accomplish. Maybe I could create a little questionnaire.

Then I remembered I'd have to leave a lot of space for answers. "What if he wanted to change everything about himself?"

He glanced at me. "Everything? Then I'd probably work on helping him like himself as he was."

"But . . . what if he was, say, super-nerdy and couldn't talk to a girl without stammering and turning bright red?"

He laughed. "I don't know. Maybe changing how he looks would help build his confidence. Make him feel better about himself so that he can feel okay going up to a girl and asking her out." He stopped at my locker. It took me a minute to realize he knew exactly where my locker was. Considering that every gray locker at Freeport Academy looked the same, this was significant.

"You two are deep in conversation," Caro said, coming up behind us. The glint in her eyes was back. "Walk me to French, will you, Sam? I'm going to bomb the test. I'm completely lost when it comes to the past-tense conjugations. You can whisper them in my ear on the way."

Caro had removed the ballet-style wrap cardigan she'd been wearing that morning. She had on a tiny tight microfiber tank top. And Sam clearly liked it. He couldn't take his eyes off her.

"Bye, Madeline," she called over her shoulder.

As I watched them walk away, she turned back and shot me a famous Caro look, which said, *Don't even think about it.*

During study hall, I created my questionnaire on one of the computers and printed three copies.

Name: _____

What do you most want to change about yourself?

Why do you want to change?

What do you think will be the hardest thing about transforming yourself into the you-est you that you can be?

Note: Forms will be kept strictly confidential.

I stole that "you-est you" part from my aunt Darcy and my mom. I didn't really understand it, actually. If you wanted to change, totally change, transform from a nobody into a somebody, from most Not to Most, why would you want to be even more *you*? I put in the fine print about confidentiality because I wanted the interns to be really honest.

Elinor and I exchanged papers before gym class: I gave her the questionnaires to hand out, and she gave me a proposed schedule. The interns wanted to meet twice a week for four weeks, starting the next day. We'd meet for one hour at the farm after their shift on Wednesdays, and on Saturday mornings at one of their houses. A quick calculation told me I was earning fifty bucks an hour. Not bad.

In gym, Elinor missed three easy volleyball shots and then ended up practically breaking her nose while diving onto her stomach to hit the ball. She still missed it, and then it landed on her back.

"God, could you be more of a total dork?" someone said to her, and everyone in hearing distance laughed.

Except me. Elinor looked like she was about to burst into tears. The girl next to Elinor helped her up, but Elinor's knee was so bruised she was excused from the rest of class.

As she hobbled away, there were giggled whispers of "What a loser."

I felt bad for her. I'd never had to deal with anything like that before I became part of the popular crowd. I was just ignored—not picked on. And once I became popular, I was so focused on my friends that I never paid much attention to anyone else.

Like Elinor.

I just waltzed down the halls with Caro, Fergie, Annie, and Selena, oblivious to anyone else.

But really . . . why was I popular? Was it just because I was Thom Geller's girlfriend? Or was it because I intimidated everyone the way my friends did? If I came to school with no makeup, flat hair, and ugly clothes, would I suddenly not be me anymore?

Caro would say it was Elinor's fault for being such a total loser in the first place. That her dorkiness had everything to do with her. But if no one picked on her, she wouldn't *be* a loser. She'd just be Elinor, being herself. Why couldn't that be okay?

On the ride home from school, I posed that very question to Caro and Fergie.

"Omigod, Madeline, you are boring me to death," Caro said, rolling her eyes and glancing out the window.

"It is kind of boring, Madeline," Fergie added as

she scrolled through her messages. "I mean, there is nothing to debate. It is what it is." She tossed her phone into her bag. "I love that expression, don't you?"

It is what it is.

But it didn't have to be.

Chapter 8

On Saturday, my mom gave me a ride to Elinor's house. "Honey, did you speak to your dad about the wedding?" she asked. "Is he planning to book your and Sabrina's flight?"

"Actually he said he couldn't afford the tickets," I told her. Sabrina hadn't said I couldn't tell the truth, just that I shouldn't ask for my mom to pay my way.

Please offer, please offer, please offer, I prayed. Then I could cancel this . . . *thing* with the interns and spend the rest of the month dreaming of California, dreaming of Thom.

The night before, he'd called and we'd talked for an entire hour about his life, my life. And how much we missed each other. How much he missed the perfume I always wore. After we hung up, I just lay on my bed and closed my eyes and saw nothing but Thom. Once again, everything was forgotten. Caro's beyotchiness. The itty-bitty crush I was developing on Sam—which clearly couldn't be real. And the interns. I really wanted to forget them.

"I wish I could swing it," my mom said, reaching over to smooth my hair. "But everything has gone up this year. We're barely going to break even."

Now I felt like the brat my sister always accused me of being. My mom and Mac were so good to me. They let me be me, even though that meant I hated everything about their lives and their dream—the farm. They never teased me about thinking I was Ms. Sophisticated, the way Sabrina did. I had to say, I was pretty lucky when it came to my mom and my stepfather. "That's okay, Mom," I said, my heart twisting. "I actually got a job. A weird job, but a job. A few of the interns have hired me to give them advice on how to be more popular and make themselves over. Like what I learned in Rome."

She glanced at me. "They're paying you?"

"It was their idea," I said quickly. "If I didn't need the money for the ticket, I wouldn't have said yes."

"Still, Madeline, that's—"

"Mom, the way they dress and act at the farm is how they dress and act all the time. Elinor is tortured at school on a regular basis just for being herself."

"I see. So you're going to teach her and the others how not to be themselves?"

"Not *not* themselves, just not so . . . torture-able."

She raised an eyebrow. "Well, it'll be an interesting study, anyway." She pulled into Elinor's driveway. "Call if you need a ride home," she said. She blew me a kiss, then drove off.

And left me in front of Elinor Espinoza's house. Which meant I really and truly had to do this, had to help them. *Count to five. Okay.*

I raised my hand to ring the doorbell, but Elinor opened the front door before I could.

"Elinor, you shouldn't be so . . . eager," I said. "Wait for the knock. Count to five, *then* answer the door."

"Why?" she asked. "I heard your car pull up. I was expecting you. Why not greet you?"

"Because, that's why. You don't want someone to think that you weren't doing something else. That you weren't busy."

She furrowed her thick eyebrows. "Why would I be busy? If I was expecting you?"

"Just wait for the knock next time, okay?"

"You're the Most," she said, "so okay."

Oh God. For a while there, I'd thought that this wouldn't be so bad, that it wouldn't be so hard. Clearly it would be torture.

"Everyone's here," she said, leading the way up the stairs.

Elinor's bedroom looked exactly the same as it

had the last time I'd been over: really girly—the opposite of Elinor. Pale pink walls and pink and white ruffles on everything, from the curtains to the bedding to the rug, which had pink and white hearts.

Joe was at her desk, by the window, looking like he wanted to flee at any second. He wore a dorky striped polo shirt, bright blue and yellow, tucked into khaki pants. And huge white athletic sneakers that even my mom had stopped buying for herself like five years ago.

Avery sat on a pink beanbag under a framed poster of a fluffy white cat. She had on okay jeans and a yellow T-shirt with ruffles around the neck. Nothing that Fergie would ever wear, but nothing I hadn't seen on some of the popular girls. She had standard hair, straight to the shoulders, with bangs that could use a little edge, maybe, but it was perfectly cute. With a little more makeup and better shoes, she'd look great. With her, it wasn't about the clothes. It was something else. I just hadn't put my finger on it yet.

"Hi," I said. "Um, so . . . does everyone have their forms filled out?"

They all reached into their knapsacks and handed me their sheets.

"So, are you all okay with me reading them aloud?" I asked. "Or do you want to keep them confidential?"

"I'm okay with reading mine aloud," Elinor said. "But I don't mind if you guys want to keep yours private."

"I'm okay with it too," Avery said. "We're all here for the same reason, more or less."

Was that a little zing at Elinor and Joe for needing more work than she did? If it was, Elinor and Joe didn't seem to pick up on it. Maybe I was just so trained at noting and decoding sarcasm and snarkiness.

"Um, I'm not sure I want mine read," Joe said. "Not that it says anything you guys don't already know, but . . . I don't know."

"You were honest in the questionnaire?" Elinor asked. "Maybe more than you planned to be?"

His cheeks reddened and he nodded. "I guess seeing the questions in black and white like that really made me think about this stuff. I mean, *really* think about it. I get called a dork all the time, but I'm not even sure why, you know? I don't get what I'm doing so wrong. That's the problem, though, I guess," he added with a nervous laugh.

"That is the problem for all of us," Avery said. "We don't get what we're doing wrong. But Madeline totally knows that. Firsthand." She stared at me. "You were a total nobody in eighth grade. And then you transformed yourself into one of the most popular girls at school. I want to know your secrets."

"Ooh, me too!" Elinor said. "Not that I expect to be voted Miss Popularity anytime soon."

"You never know," Avery said, running her hands through her fine brown hair.

Note to self: watch Avery like a hawk. There was something just slightly "I'm going to strangle you in your sleep" about her.

I glanced around the room for somewhere to sit. The only place left was the padded white bench next to Elinor's vanity. I sat down and felt everyone's eyes on me. Yup, they were all staring. Talk about pressure. "Okay, so I'm just going to read through the forms—out loud. But not Joe's."

Name: Elinor Espinoza
_____

What do you most want to change about yourself?
Everything. How I look, how shy I am around people.

Why do you want to change?
I don't want to be a Not again.

What do you think will be the hardest thing about transforming yourself into the you-est you that you can be?
Sometimes I think I'm just stuck like this, that this is the me-est me.
P.S. I'm also planning to try out for the Lobster

Claw Teen Queen Pageant, and I think a head-to-toe makeover would really help me. My stepmother won when she was a teenager, but every time she tries to suggest things to make me look better, I just want to kill her. She thinks I'm hopeless, I know. If I can just place and get her off my back, I'd be happier, I think.

"Omigod, Elinor," Avery said. "That's so sad about your stepmother. That must be really hard."

"It's not so bad," Elinor said. "I only see her every other weekend, when I go to my dad's."

"All the more reason she should accept you as you are," Joe put in.

I thought about telling her about Tiffany, my soon-to-be second stepmother, who I wouldn't meet until the wedding. I had no idea if Tiffany even liked teenagers or had any interest in me and Sabrina. She didn't seem to.

But I didn't really want to share details of my life with this group. They already knew too much about me. I wondered if Elinor had told Avery all about how I used to be a nobody with no friends. I could see her saying it in a totally unsnarky way, just to illustrate that I had experience in what they were paying big bucks for.

"You know what?" Joe said, tugging his shirt collar. "You can read my form out loud."

"Go, Joe!" Elinor said with her accompanying little claps.

Okay, I had to say something. Enough with the dorky clapping and jumping. "Um, Elinor, I just thought I should tell you that clapping like that isn't really something you'd see the popular girls doing. Except the cheerleaders during a game."

Her cheeks reddened. "Oh. Oh! That's great—thank you so much, Madeline. It's exactly the kind of thing I need to know." She reached onto her desk for a little notebook and jotted something down. *No clapping,* I assumed.

"It's just a little too much," I added. "It's great to be happy for someone or happy period. Just don't overdo it."

"This is just perfect," Elinor said, writing furiously.

"Okay, Joe," I said. I had no idea what to expect from his form.

Name: *Joe (Joseph) Georgeoff*

What do you most want to change about yourself?
I really don't know. See why below.

Why do you want to change?
Is this confidential? If it is, the answer is that I like someone and right now she doesn't even know I exist. No girl's ever been into me before, so I figure

she's not, so I'm not exactly okay with just talking to her or anything, but I want to.

What do you think will be the hardest thing about transforming yourself into the you-est you that you can be?
I don't know. Why aren't any girls into me? Is it how I look? Do I smell?

"You totally don't smell," Elinor said to Joe.

Except faintly of cow. But they *all* did.

"Oooh, so who do you like?" Avery asked, her blue eyes twinkling.

Joe's cheeks were now flaming. "Um, can that part be confidential?" he asked me. "I mean, it's no one in this room, if that makes it less weird." Now his whole face was really red. "Not that you're all not . . . I mean . . ."

"Joe, totally confidential," I said before he spontaneously combusted. "Anything that anyone wants to keep to themselves is okay."

I was feeling better about this. I'd forgotten how good it felt to help people. And to have people appreciate me—for doing something good. For doing anything other than walking down the hall.

"You know, Joe," Elinor said, "I'll bet girls have been interested in you. But because you keep to yourself and walk with your head down a lot, you're kind of unapproachable. Do you think that could be it, Madeline?"

"Definitely," I said. "That was really good, Elinor."

"Ditto," Avery said, eyeing me.

"Okay. Whew," Joe said. "That wasn't so bad, then. I guess maybe agreeing to do this was a good idea."

I smiled at him and he perked up a little.

"Okay, now Avery," I said. I couldn't wait to read hers. She'd been pretty honest so far.

Name: *Avery Kennar*

What do you most want to change about yourself?
how people see me

Why do you want to change?
make friends, be more popular, get a boyfriend I'm crazy about

What do you think will be the hardest thing about transforming yourself into the you-est you that you can be?
Getting people to see me. It's like I'm invisible. Even when I try to glam up, no one seems to notice. What am I doing wrong? How am I supposed to become more popular if no one knows who I am? I wish I knew the secret.

"Well, now you will," Elinor said to Avery. "That's what Madeline is going to share with us. The secrets. How she did it."

"I'm totally ready," Avery said. "I want to start now so I can have an amazing summer and start my junior year off a brand-new person."

They all turned to me expectantly. Waiting for my Most wisdom.

After reading all their forms and listening to them, I knew what I had to do.

Return their money.

First of all, Elinor wanted to enter the Lobster Claw Teen Queen Pageant? That was Caro's territory. So forget about helping Elinor win or even place. And Joe—what did I know about transforming a guy, anyway? Then there was Avery, who might be the hardest one, because she was actually kind of cute in a bland way. She just clearly had no confidence. How was I supposed to change *that*? In four weeks!

Do you want to get to California or not? I reminded myself.

"Can I ask you something?" Joe said. He was staring at me with puppy dog eyes and that hopeful smile.

"Sure."

"Just off the top of your head, what would you say is the main thing I'm doing wrong? I mean, just

93

by looking at me. Knowing that alone would give me my money's worth."

I read through his form again, then looked him over. He was very skinny and didn't have much of a chin, but he had really nice blue eyes. His clothes were dorky—tucked-in striped polo shirt and weird-colored khakis. This was how he dressed on a Saturday? Or ever?

"Well, actually, Joe, I think we do need to start with the outside of all of you," I said. "Makeovers change how you look on the outside, so you'll feel better about yourself on the inside. That'll give you all more confidence. Confidence is the key."

At least, that was what Aunt Darcy had told me in Rome.

"So, Joe, untuck that shirt," I said. "That will make a big difference."

"But won't I look sloppy? That's what my mom says when I walk around the house untucked."

"You won't look sloppy at all. At school tomorrow, look at every guy you see. Tell me how many wear their shirts tucked in."

He brightened with his social assignment.

I suddenly had an idea. "Experiment time," I said. "Elinor, I'm going to switch outfits with you. Let's go into the bathroom and change."

Behind closed doors, we faced away from each other and traded tops. Elinor's boring navy T-shirt with a pocket felt heavy after the pale yellow cotton tank top I'd just taken off. We exchanged bottoms— her dark gray track pants for my Sevens. Her sneakers were a little tight but I squeezed my feet into them. She took off her white socks with the dumb kiddie pom-poms on the backs and slipped into my favorite Caro castoffs, glittery and strappy flat metallic sandals that tied up the ankle.

The jeans could be a little tighter (Elinor was a stick), but she looked . . . better. Something wasn't quite right, though. Maybe I needed to study her from more of a distance. "Okay, let's go show everyone what we look like."

When we stepped out, everyone was frowning. Elinor opened her closet door, where a full-length mirror hung.

"She looks cute, but I don't know, those jeans just aren't her. They're too . . . something," Avery said.

"Sexy," I put in. "They're a little loose, but she still looks hot in them. And that's not a bad thing. We're just not used to seeing Elinor that way."

"Elinor isn't used to seeing Elinor that way," Elinor said. "Wow," she added, glancing at herself in the mirror. "But there is no way I could ever wear something like this in public. It just isn't me."

"Isn't that the point?" I asked. "To change your image?"

"Yeah," Elinor said. "But I couldn't just show up

at school wearing these jeans and a skimpy little tank—no offense."

"Okay, fine," I said. "Then tell me how I look." I faced everyone in the T-shirt and track pants and sneakers.

"Your hair doesn't go with that outfit," Elinor said. "You should pull it up in a ponytail."

"But you weren't wearing a ponytail, Elinor," Avery pointed out.

"Exactly," I said. "So there's a mismatch going on between her hair and the clothes she wears. Now you're seeing what everyone else sees."

"You don't look bad, necessarily," Avery said. "Just like you're going running."

Elinor studied me. "But she's not. I guess that's the point too."

"What was going through your mind when you put this on?" I asked her.

She eyed her closet. "I just wanted to be comfortable."

"Is what you're wearing right now comfortable?" I asked.

"Actually, yeah. Even the shoes are," she said.

"So you could have chosen a cute tank top, trendy jeans, and cute sandals and you would have been just as comfortable and looked great instead of like you were going running."

Elinor laughed. "I guess so. But I still couldn't

imagine picking this outfit for a Saturday hanging out at home."

"I live on a farm and chose this outfit," I reminded her.

"She has you there," Joe said.

"Before I went to Rome, I never would have worn clothes like this. I'd see them in a store and think they were cute but I didn't think I could wear them. My aunt helped me realize that you should wear what makes you feel good."

"But my clothes *do* make me feel good," Elinor said. "That's the problem."

That *was* a problem. One I didn't have the solution to. Yet, anyway.

We changed back into our own clothes.

"I'm dying to know what you think I should do with myself," Avery said.

I studied her. "I think if you wear the clothes, put on just a little makeup, like one coat of mascara and some lip gloss, you'll look really polished."

"The problem is that I can't afford new clothes," she said. "I spent everything I had on this class."

"I can let you borrow a few things," I said. "You can go through my closet next time."

She brightened. "Really? Thanks."

I nodded. "So, Joe, back to you. Come look in the mirror." He leaped up. "Okay, see how much better that looks already? You never want to tuck a

97

polo shirt in. I'll pay closer attention tomorrow to what guys are wearing. But you should too."

"Okay," he said. "Improved already."

"And your hair," I said. "The part is too . . . parted. Try messing it up a little."

He shoved his hand into his hair and gave it a vigorous shake. "Like this?"

"Hey, that looks good," Elinor said. "Wow."

"I'm *not* using hair gunk," Joe said. "You weren't about to tell me I had to, were you?"

Sigh. Thom used hair gel. "Totally up to you. Just a tiny bit can give your hair a little edge. Try it, really."

He raised an eyebrow. "Maybe."

"Well, I'd say our first class was a total success," Elinor said, restraining herself from clapping. "Let's celebrate with lunch. My mom is making something for us."

Huh? No one had said anything about *lunch.* Or socializing past the agreed-upon hour-long meeting. "Um, Elinor, I'm actually meeting my friends, so—"

Elinor blushed. "Oh. Okay. Well, see you Wednesday, then. I mean, I'll see you before Wednesday, like at the farm. And school. But you know what I mean."

I was starting to feel kind of bad for her. Did I make her that nervous? She talked to me the way I used to try to talk to some of the popular kids at school, like Annie, when she blew me off. And like Thom that first day he spoke to me. That was weird—making someone feel that nervous.

"So where do you guys hang out?" Avery asked me nonchalantly as she dug around in her purse and pulled out a thin tube of lip gloss. "Besides the Coffee Connection and Yum's and the stone bench in the atrium at school. Those are the only places I ever see you."

"Those are our places," I said. "We usually hang out at each other's houses."

"Oh," she said, slicking on the dark pink lip gloss. "Is it always you and Caro and Fergie and Selena and Annie? You guys seem very tight. Do you ever hang out with other people?"

"Sometimes," I said. "We have other friends, and sometimes we'll end up with a really big group. But yeah, the five of us are close." I wanted to get out of this room, out of this house, really bad. I made a show of looking at my watch. "Ooh, I'd better go. See you next time."

I was heading down the path when Elinor came running after me. "Wait," she said, handing me an envelope with my name on it. "There's the first half. Two hundred dollars. I counted it twice. It's all there. And you'll have the next two hundred in two weeks—I promise."

"Thanks," I said, and tucked the envelope into my bag. It felt so good to have it, to know it was there.

Once I was on my way, I let out the deep breath I hadn't realized I'd been holding.

When I arrived at Yum's, no one was there yet, which was weird, because I was ten minutes late. Elinor's house was a fifteen-minute walk to downtown, but I hadn't wanted to ask Caro to pick me up on her way. I glanced around the not-too-busy casual restaurant again. No sign of any of them. So I stood in the waiting area and checked my phone for texts. Just one, but a good one: *Miss you. T.*

Five minutes later, I was still standing there. Had I gotten the time wrong? Place? I called Caro's cell, but it went straight to her voice mail. I left a message that I was there and waiting. Then I called Fergie's cell. Straight to voice mail. That was definitely odd.

I waited another fifteen minutes and then tried both their cells again. Straight to voice mail. What was going on?

I turned to leave and stopped dead in my tracks. Caro, Fergie, Annie, Selena, and Morgan, Thom's girlfriend before me, were heading into Coffee Connection across the street. Caro, Fergie, and Morgan were laughing as they went in. And Selena and Annie were deep in conversation steps behind them.

My stomach twisted with that creepy, scary, nausea-producing feeling. Had they forgotten about lunch? But why not answer their phones? They all checked their messages five times a minute. Why didn't anyone call me back?

And what was Morgan suddenly doing with them? She and her cheerleader friends sometimes came to our parties, and we went to theirs, but Morgan had never hung out with us alone.

Caro was trying to tell me something. And I had no idea what.

Chapter 9

I called home to see if someone could pick me up. Since my mom and Mac were out in the pastures, Sabrina grumbled that she'd come get me.

Ugh. What I wanted was my mom. Or even Mac. They always gave me space when they could tell that something was wrong. Sabrina would demand to know what could be causing a frown in my perfect little life, and I wasn't in the mood to get picked on. I'd told her to pick me up in front of the post office, around the corner from Yum's and Coffee Connection. I didn't want my friends to see me slinking out of Yum's like a loser.

When I saw Sabrina behind the wheel of my mom's Subaru, I darted out and around the corner and into the passenger seat.

"You get weirder every day," my sister said, a

cap made of hemp on her head. "Let me guess. A geek was coming toward you and you didn't want to have to talk to her."

"Whatever, I'm not in the mood," I said, and stared out the window as she pulled away from the curb. What was going on with Caro? What was she trying to tell me? That hanging out with the farm freaks and daring to talk to Sam would get me iced out of the group?

"So what's this about you helping the interns find their inner popularity?" Sabrina asked, digging in the console cup for a malt ball. She popped it into her mouth and crunched.

I crossed my arms over my chest. "They're paying my way to Dad's wedding."

"Unbelievable," she said around the malt ball. "An airline ticket to California costs what, five hundred bucks?"

"Three hundred something. They're paying me four hundred to be safe."

My sister took her eyes off the road to stare at me. "And what are you delivering for four hundred dollars? How to be more like you? God help them."

"Now I won't feel so guilty when I tell Dad I want to live with him," I snapped. Uh-oh. I wasn't supposed to say that out loud. Yet.

"Maddie, you're delusional if you think Dad will

let you live with him. All he cares about is Tiffany. You think she wants her teenaged stepdaughter emoting all over her precious fancy beach condo?"

"We'll see," I said confidently. But she could be right. If I didn't ask, I wouldn't know for sure. That made a difference between getting what you wanted and not: *asking*.

Sabrina did her trademarked head shake. "What do Mom and Mac have to say about this?"

"I haven't mentioned it to them yet. And anyway, I'm just thinking about it. But I'm sure they'll understand why I'm thinking about it. It's not like I fit in here."

"You don't fit in," she said. *"Right."*

"At home, I mean. At the farm. At dinner. In the family room. You and Mom and Mac love the farm. Love getting woken up by roosters and side-stepping cow dung. You want to work with farm animals for life, Sabrina. And you guys are happy to talk about it all night long after spending hours grooming cows and raking poop. *I* want what I had in Rome with Aunt Darcy. I want to feel like that every day."

"Like what?" she asked.

"Like . . . happy. Like waking up in the morning and jumping out of bed because I'm so excited to get up. Like going to bed feeling like someone sprinkled fairy dust on me because I'm so, I don't know, *fulfilled*. I felt amazing there, Sabrina. I felt *right*."

She was quiet for a moment. "That's how *everyone* wants to feel, Maddie. That's all anyone wants. You have to find it where you are. Running away to California isn't going to change anything. Haven't you ever heard that saying 'Wherever you go, there you are'?"

"*'There'* has Thom."

"Thom wasn't in Rome when you felt so fulfilled and happy and right."

"Duh, Sabrina, we weren't a couple then."

"I'm just saying he's not going to make or break your happiness."

"Whatever. I'm going to Dad's wedding. I'm going to see Thom again and everything's going to be just like always between us. Even if I don't stay, we'll reconnect and it'll keep us going until he can fly to Maine or I can get back to California."

She glanced at me with a raised eyebrow. "Maddie, come on. I'd be surprised if you two didn't break up before the week was over. And I'm not saying that to be a bitch. I'm just being honest. You're on opposite coasts. And both of you are sickeningly like rock stars in your little high school worlds. Neither of you will be single for long."

"Unless we *want* to stay together," I snapped.

"Why would we break up? We've been together for *two years,* remember?"

"And you really think you'll stay together forever?"

"I don't know, yeah."

"Maddie, do you really think Thom Geller doesn't have a new girlfriend already? Homecoming princess or whatever? I just hate to see you banking your hopes on this big love reunion only to get hurt—especially after shelling out four hundred bucks to get there. It's not like Daddy Dearest or Tiffassley will comfort you or give a flying fig."

She was infuriating. If the car hadn't been going so fast, I'd have jumped out. "First of all, it's homecoming *queen.* And second, you don't know anything about me or Thom, Sabrina, so just shut up about us, okay? I don't have a new boyfriend. So what makes you so sure he has a new girlfriend?"

"Because guys are different than girls, my dear. You know it's true, so don't get all politically correct on me."

She's not necessarily right, I told myself. Thom texted me all the time. He was still my boyfriend. There was no homecoming queen in a pink bikini wrapping her arms around his neck right that minute. "Whatever, Sabrina. Anyway, Thom's not the *only* reason I want to go to California. I *do* want to go to our father's wedding. And I need to get away from the farm and from my fr—" I cut my-self off.

"Your friends? Interesting. Too mean for you?"

Ugh. Ugh. Ugh. "Why am I even talking to you?"

"Because, Maddie, you *know* I don't want to see my delusional kid sister get smashed to smithereens. I can't stand your friends, but you're not bad, most of the time."

"Gee, thanks."

She laughed and I rolled my eyes and stared out the window and stewed. God, she was unbearable and annoying.

But she also lived the life of the interns. She was one of them. She could actually be of use during this interminable car ride home.

"So enough with the lecture and tell me some-thing, Sabrina. If you were paying me to help you become more like me, what would you really want to know?"

She turned onto Flying Point Road. Good, I'd be home and free of her in three minutes. "Can I make sarcastic comments or do I have to be earnest?"

"Sabrina, just be *normal* for once. Please."

"Fine," she said. "That is exactly what I'd want to know. How to seem more normal to other peo-ple and still be me."

"So you wouldn't necessarily want to change at all? Just *seem* different?"

"Everyone wants to be accepted, Maddie." And with that, she popped another malt ball into her mouth and turned onto our dirt driveway.

I checked for messages from Caro or Fergie. None.

Okay. What was going on?

I called Caro again, my heart thudding. What was I so nervous about? It was possible I'd gotten the time or the place wrong. But I knew I hadn't.

Caro picked up. I hadn't expected that, so I froze and went mute. *Say something, idiot!*

"Madeline?"

"Um, yeah, hi. So what happened with lunch? I waited at Yum's and no one showed."

"Oh, sorry," she said. "We changed our plans. Didn't anyone call you?"

My stomach twisted again. "No, no one called me. And no one called me back after I left messages."

"Well, whatever," she said. "Ooh, gotta go. Morgan is showing me the earrings her new boyfriend gave her last night. Talk to you later."

Click.

So. Just in case I hadn't seen her with Morgan, she was making sure I knew. And making sure I knew that Morgan wasn't talking up the guy Caro wanted, because Morgan already had an earring-giving boyfriend.

So was that what this was about? The Sam thing? Or was she annoyed that I'd spent an hour of my life at Elinor Espinoza's house and now had cooties or something?

Either way, I didn't feel sprinkled with fairy dust at the moment.

Chapter 10

On Monday, I went to "our spot" before home-room, but no one was there. Actually, someone was there. Avery Kennar. Where were my friends?

Okay, this was going too far. First Yum's and now the bench? Caro and Fergie and I met at the stone bench in the atrium before homeroom every morning.

"Hi, Madeline," Avery said. She was sitting right in the middle of the bench, as though she belonged there. No one but us sat on that bench. Ever. Except the popular guys, and only if we weren't using it. But Avery wouldn't know that. She was still pretty new.

"So I tried a new combination today," she said, standing up. "Do you think these pants are okay?"

Go away, I wanted to scream. I just wanted to sit here in peace and figure out if my friends were shut-ting me out or if this was just another coincidence.

Right. The first time in two years Caro and Fergie weren't at the bench. After shutting me out of lunch on Saturday. Not a coincidence.

"Madeline?"

"You look fine," I muttered.

"Is something wrong?" she asked.

"Yes. And I don't want to talk about it."

I walked away from the building toward a cluster of shrubs and burst into tears. And of course Avery had followed me.

"Here's a tissue," she said, handing me one. "Your mascara's not running." She held up her little gold compact so I could see.

"Thanks," I said, dabbing under my eyes.

"Having problems with your friends?" she asked. "I mean, I know you guys usually meet here in the mornings."

So she did know. Interesting. Then what had she been doing sitting there in the middle of the bench?

Maybe that was why Caro and Fergie hadn't shown up. They'd seen Avery there and figured I'd told her to meet me there or something.

"Did you see Caro and Fergie this morning?"

She shook her head. "I mean, I did see them by their lockers like a few minutes ago. With Selena McFarland and Annie Something and a few other girls. But then they went in the other direction, toward the cafeteria."

Ah. So it wasn't about Avery.

"Things are just a little weird right now," I said. "Everything feels so up in the air, you know?"

Now I was telling my life story to Avery? I had to stop.

She handed me another tissue. "I've felt like that since I moved here. It's the worst feeling."

I nodded. It was how I'd felt the year before I started going out with Thom. Before I became friends with Caro.

I took a deep breath. "Can I borrow your compact again?" She handed it to me and I made sure I looked okay. Nose not red. Eyeliner not running down my cheeks.

She put the compact back into her messenger bag. "Do you think if I took off this sweater and tied it around my hips, I'd look better?" she asked, unbuttoning the blue cardigan.

Just then, Tate and Ceej and Sam walked by and Tate whistled at Avery as she removed the sweater. She wore a little white tank top. I could see the outline of her bra.

She smiled at the guys as Tate wolf-whistled again before they disappeared around the corner. "Guess I *do* look better," she said.

Thank God Caro and Fergie weren't here for *that*.

• • •

Caro, Fergie, Annie, and Selena were waiting for me by my locker as usual when the lunch bell rang. Now I felt like I'd imagined the weirdness on Saturday and that morning. I'd tried to ask Caro about it a few times, but she'd either brushed me off or we'd been interrupted by Selena or Annie or one of the other countless girls who worshipped Caro.

Caro complimented my shoes, which I'd bought on Sunday because I'd been so depressed. I'd called Thom twice that day and he hadn't called me back till late that night. He'd never forgotten the time zone difference before. My mom heard my phone ring and came in and told me I could talk for one minute only, because it was so late.

He was in his new world, living his life.

"So where were you this morning?" I asked Caro and Fergie. Selena and Annie were their usual foot behind. I wasn't just going to pretend that that morning hadn't happened.

Caro and Fergie shared a glance; then Caro slowly turned her attention to me. "Fergie and I were discussing something important. So we didn't get a chance to meet up at the bench."

"Like what?" I asked.

"Guess who was asking about you today, Madeline," Fergie said as we headed into the caf. In other words, neither of them was going to answer my question.

"Who?" I asked.

"James McNeil. God, he is hot. I'm so into Tate that I barely notice other guys, but when I was talking to James, I couldn't believe how good-looking he is."

"He asked me about you too," Caro said, placing a salad on her tray. "If you've hooked up with anyone yet. I told him no, and you should have seen his smile. Has he asked you out yet?"

"No and I'm not interested," I told her, my appetite gone. "I'm going to see Thom in two and a half weeks when I fly out to California. We're *still* together, you know."

"Sweetie, I'm just being realistic," Caro said.

Fergie stared at the rows of cheeseburgers, which of course she wouldn't select. She went for the salad too. "And come on, Madeline. I mean, you and Thom were a couple for two years, so there's obviously something there. But he's gone. And if you're suddenly hanging out with the farm freaks and thinking you can help them, you are so not facing reality."

"Then again, it's not like she can make the farm freaks worse," Annie said, and cracked up. "There's nowhere to go but up."

Bitch. I glared at her, and her smile faded. She grabbed a container of french fries.

What did my friends and I used to talk about? Suddenly, I couldn't remember. I never had to say much. I just fit in because of how I looked and because of Thom.

Now he was gone.

And there didn't seem to be much me in this crowd without him—or another him. As long as that other him wasn't Sam Fray.

"So how are things with the farm freaks, anyway?" Selena asked, also placing a salad on her tray.

"They just want to fit in," I said.

We handed over our lunch cards; then Caro led the way to our table. "You're either normal or you're not. You don't just become normal by wearing good jeans. Though Frizz Puff would look a lot better if she straightened her hair."

This was typical Caro. Everything was okay again. I didn't know why, but it was. "Well, that's the kind of thing I'm doing. Helping them make improvements so they'll fit in. Like with clothes and—"

"Wait," Selena said. "You're actually hanging out with them? Like in public? Like you're going to the mall with them to shop?"

Well, not yet. But so what? I wanted to scream. I was so sick of this. Elinor and Avery and Joe were just people. They weren't aliens. To be honest, I wouldn't exactly be comfortable hanging at the mall with them, but I *owed* them a mall trip, so I'd have to get over it. "We're mostly just meeting at their houses," I explained.

"I'd wear sunglasses and put my hair up in a really cool hat," Fergie said. "You don't want anyone to see you."

I didn't, actually. But part of me didn't really care. Now that I'd sort of gotten to know them, they weren't as freaky. "But won't the interns know I'm trying to be incognito because of them?"

"So?" Caro said. "They're farm freaks. They'll understand."

Annie burst out laughing.

I let out a silent sigh and checked my cell. No texts from Thom.

Things seemed to be okay with my friends for now. But not with Thom.

To: MadGirl@maine.com
From: TGeller@cal.com
Hey, sorry crazy busy. Talk 2morrow or next day. Just 2¹/₂ more weeks! XX T

I texted back right away, but he didn't respond. So confusing.

Chapter 11

Wednesday's class started out in my bedroom, with Elinor going through my closet to see what clothes caught her eye. I was trying to develop her "personal style," something I'd read about in *Seventeen*. The gist of the article was that to have personal style, you had to create a look that was uniquely you.

"Ooh, I like this, and that, oh, and this!" she said, grabbing shirts and pants and skirts and laying them over her arm. "Oooh, and this!"

Okay, so Elinor liked bright colors. I supposed that could be uniquely her.

"Okay, Avery, your turn. Just pick three outfits you like, stuff you can mix and match with your own clothes."

Avery picked all the hand-me-downs I'd gotten

from Caro. Good taste. She came out of the bathroom in tight Citizen jeans, a ruffled white sleeveless top, and high-heeled mules.

"Double wow," Elinor said.

"Definitely wow," Joe said, "if I can say that without sounding like a pig."

"Seriously wow," I added, looking at her reflection in the mirror. "You look amazing. You look like you belong in those clothes."

"I guess I just needed access to them," she said, turning left and right and checking out the rear view in the mirror. "My family isn't exactly rich."

"Well, you're definitely on your way to getting what you want," I said. "Some makeup and maybe some hair gel and you're done, Avery."

"No way, she needs some attitude," Elinor said.

I glanced at Avery, who was still checking herself out in the mirror, her expression . . . *satisfied*. Very satisfied.

I had the feeling that Avery Kennar had enough attitude. She just needed the clothes to give her the right to it.

"To the mall for makeovers!" Elinor said. "It's so strange—I *could* have gotten a makeover anytime. I mean, I *could* have gone to the mall for a haircut with someone who specializes in curly hair. I *could* have gotten my face done at a makeup counter. I *could* have asked the salesgirls in Forever 21 to help me pick out a few outfits. But I never *felt* like I could. And now I do." She was about to jump and clap, but then looked at me and grinned. "Caught myself!"

I smiled at her. She was goofy, but sort of endearing in her own way. I wondered, though, about what she'd said. She could have gotten a makeover anytime. A total head-to-toe makeover. Just like I'd told her when she'd first tried to bribe me with a hundred dollars.

So why was now different?

Elinor's father drove us. I sat up front with Mr. Espinoza, who hummed the entire way to South Portland. He dropped us off at Macy's. It was weird getting out of the car for a mall run with Elinor, Avery, and Joe. Very surreal. I kept my oversized sunglasses on when we headed inside.

But I could barely see anything, so I shoved them into my purse. We made our way to my favorite cosmetics counter—MAC—and we girls all got makeovers, me included, not that I looked much different. Elinor's skin glowed and her dark eyes seemed brighter. She wiped off three-quarters of what was applied to her face, but kept the mascara and the lip gloss. Avery looked like she was twenty-five with makeup, so she toned it down a little. *Wow*.

"What about me?" Joe complained.

"You just need a cool haircut," I said.

As we left Macy's and headed into the mall itself, my stomach twisted. I kept expecting to run into my friends at any minute. But we didn't. I rushed the interns down the wing that housed Hair Flair. An hour later, Avery's shoulder-length brown hair had been transformed into a style like Fergie's, an A-line bob with model-like bangs. Elinor's frizz was slightly controlled and fell into frizzy ringlets, but at least the horizontal frizz puffs were gone.

"I look awesome!" Elinor said, checking herself out in the mirror. "Omigod. I didn't think my hair could look like this!"

"Avery, you look like a model!" Joe said, jaw to the floor.

She did, actually. If Tate thought she was hot before, in just a tank top, wait till he saw this.

"You are definitely earning your money, Madeline," Avery said. "We look like different people."

And they were acting like different people too. Not so much in personality, but in confidence. Elinor walked through the mall with her head up, not down as usual. She couldn't keep her hands off her ringlets. And Joe, with his tousled and spiky cut and untucked T-shirt and cargo pants, looked great— and like most of the guys at Freeport Academy. And Avery—wow. The most incredible transformation of all. Much like my own had been. She'd gone from perfectly okay plain girl to model-hot chic.

Success.

Elinor's father wasn't picking us up for another half hour, so Elinor suggested we head to the food court to celebrate our new looks with smoothies.

I really didn't want to turn this into hanging out at the food court. Which made me feel kind of bad again.

Avery came to my rescue. "I'm getting such a migraine," she said. "Could we just wait outside in the air?"

We all headed outside, where the May humidity had its way with Elinor's ringlets and most of our makeup. But the interns still looked amazing. It made no sense that none of them had tried something like this before. It seemed so easy.

I glanced at Elinor, who was marveling at her reflection in the shaded-glass doors. "Elinor, I'm wondering something. Before, when you said you could have gotten this done anytime, but never felt you could, why not? What's different now?"

She glanced at me and shrugged. "Permission, I guess. From who, I don't know. Myself?" She smiled. "Yeah, I guess myself."

Avery shook her head. "You're *paying* for the right to look like Madeline and her friends. The money gives you permission. You bought the right."

Elinor's smile faded. "I guess."

I glanced at Avery, who was touching up her nose with her new MAC pressed powder. That had been a little harsh. But she was right, I supposed. Still, any of them could have gone to the mall and gotten haircuts and makeovers and bought new clothes.

"I think the reason why I never changed my look before is because I didn't know it was bad," Joe said. "Yeah, I wasn't as casual as other guys, but it didn't bother me."

"You had a reason to want to change," Avery said. "Just like Elinor and me. Elinor wants to make sure her name doesn't appear on that idiotic, nasty Not list. And I want to be noticed. You want to try to attract the girl you like. It makes sense that we did something now. We all finally had reason to want to change."

That made sense. When I'd gone to Rome, I had just been glad to get away from my life. I hadn't known that I'd love sitting in cafés and people-watching. I hadn't known I'd love trying on ten white T-shirts until I found just the one and just the cute little scarf to wrap around my neck. I hadn't been exposed to that kind of stuff.

"Well, to be honest," Elinor said, "I love my hair, but I don't know how I'd maintain this myself. Did you see all that stuff the guy used on me? Like three different kinds of gels, a diffuser, and a curling iron. It's not like I'll be able to do that before school, especially on the days I have to be at the farm at the crack of dawn."

"Maybe you could just put your hair in a ponytail on your intern days. And the other days get up an hour early," Avery said.

Joe stared at us. "An hour early for hair?"

"She looks really good," Avery said. "It's worth it."

Elinor smiled and went back to marveling at the reflection of her ringlets. Joe seemed lost in thought, likely about how to ask out his dream girl. And Avery seemed very satisfied.

She leaned close. "Don't I totally look like one of your friends?" She glanced up and down her body.

"Yeah. You do," I told her.

But she didn't seem to need assuring.

Chapter 12

In school the next day, Caro stopped right in the middle of the hall. So did everyone else. "Was that the tank top I got at Kitson last summer?" she asked, staring at Avery's back. Avery, luckily for her, was halfway down the hall already.

"Actually, yes," I said. "She's borrowing it from me."

Caro stared down the hall at Avery's swinging and shiny hair. "So now you're lending the clothes I lent you," she said, her voice cold.

"The clothes you *gave* me," I pointed out. "Anything you said you didn't want back. Didn't you say that tank was 'so two summers ago'?"

"Yes, but still. I gave it to *you*. Not some stranger."

"I'm just trying to earn my airfare, Caro," I reminded her.

"Well, do it without handing out my clothes all over school," she said, resuming walking.

"And hello, was that my haircut?" Fergie asked. "Madeline, a little bit more originality, please. Now I have to change my style if everyone's going to copy me."

"You're overdue, anyway," Caro commented. Fergie shot her a look, but before she could say anything, Caro stopped dead in her tracks again. "Oh, you've got to be kidding me," she snapped as Elinor turned the corner. Elinor was dressed top to bottom in Caro Alexander hand-me-downs. "She looks ridiculous."

She sort of did, but she still looked better than she had before. And her hair looked a hundred times better.

"You have to admit it's an improvement, Caro," Fergie pointed out.

"Of course it's an *improvement,*" Caro said. "It's a Marc Jacobs skirt."

"She paired it with that orange T-shirt herself," I said. "That shows some progress, some sense of burgeoning style, don't you think?"

Caro wrinkled her face in disgust. "Why am I even talking about a *Not*?" she asked. "I *could* be telling you what happened with Sam last night. I tried to call you, Madeline, but your phone must have been shut off."

My phone had *not* been shut off. As if it would *ever* be. She was yet again making a *point*. And yet again I had no idea what it was.

"What happened with Sam?" I asked. Sam, who'd made himself scarce the past two weeks. I'd barely seen him at all. Not at the farm and not at school.

Caro leaned close. "So last night, Sam came over to help me study for the French final. And I made my move."

Fergie and I both stared at her, waiting. "I heard a little of it on the phone last night," Fergie said to me, "but Caro wanted to tell us both together."

"Well, I can't tell you in the middle of the hallway with everyone staring at me," she said. "Let's go to the bench."

We headed to the atrium. Caro texted Selena, and in ten seconds, Selena and Annie appeared at her feet. Caro liked her "girls" to surround her. Especially when she was "sharing." "Okay, so, this is what happened. We were in my bedroom, sitting on my bed, and I just took the pencil out of one of his hands and the stupid textbook out of the other, and put both his hands on my chest," she said. "While looking him right in the eye."

"Really?" I asked.

"Double really?" Fergie said.

"Yup," she said. "At first, he was so surprised he

126

didn't move a finger. But then he did. Slowly. Very slowly. And not *away*."

"And then what?" Selena asked, looking like she was about to melt onto the floor.

"And then he kissed me," Caro said. "His hands never leaving my chest. Except they went under the shirt. Under the bra."

"Omigod, that's hot," Fergie said, slicking on her sparkly red-pink lip gloss. "Then what?"

"Did you sleep with him?" I asked.

"No," Caro said. "But I might."

"Oooh!" Selena exclaimed. "Oooh, oooh, oooh!"

We were all virgins. Caro had gone the farthest. Fergie the second farthest. And me, practically nowhere. Caro had done *everything* but have sexual intercourse.

"So how far did you guys go?" Annie asked.

"Just that," Caro said. "My mom barged in like two seconds later to offer us ice cream and totally ruined the moment, and then he had to leave anyway."

"You really would have slept with him? Sex-sex?" Fergie asked.

"I think so," Caro said. "I'm not totally sure. I don't want to play my whole hand just yet."

"Meaning?" Fergie asked.

"Meaning he's clearly interested," Caro explained.

"If I give him everything he wants immediately, I'll have nothing left. C'mon, Fergie—that's Girl 101."

"So when are you seeing him again?" I asked.

She ran her fingers through her silky blond hair. "He didn't exactly ask me out. But he will. I just gave him a taste of what to expect. He'll totally want more."

"So ask *him* out," Fergie said. "Why wait for him?"

"Because I *have* been waiting," she said. "And I've made it clear I want him. If he doesn't make the next move, I'll look desperate. And desperate is not a good look for a girl."

Fergie nodded. "You should totally be voted Most Wise."

In English class, I couldn't stop looking at Sam. I kept trying to picture him making out with Caro, his hands all over her. But I couldn't.

Here was what was really weird: I felt sort of . . . jealous. But that made no sense. Well, it sort of did. I thought he liked me. And yet he went for Caro the second she put his hands on her chest.

He caught me staring and smiled at me.

And then I realized that someone was staring at me: Avery. Her hair looked amazing. She'd toned down her makeup, but she still had a model-y glow. She looked great in Caro's tank top and my old skinny jeans.

I shot her a small smile and turned my attention back to my notebook, where I scrawled *Life is really, really weird*.

Chapter 13

On Saturday, we met at Avery's house. I loved her bedroom. Everything was white and minimalist, except the cute little brown dachshund, named Lucy, on her bed.

"Guess what?" Elinor said when I sat down at Avery's desk. "I've gotten at least a hundred compliments on my hair. I can't even tell you how many girls said they wished they had long curly hair like mine! Can you believe it?" Elinor's hair didn't look like it had when she'd left the salon, but there were still defined ringlets where the mass of frizz puffs had been.

I smiled. "I can believe it. You look great."

She beamed.

Avery, unquestionably stylish, sat on her bed, and Joe was sitting against the wall. He'd gotten new sneakers. They weren't blinding white, either. He too looked great, almost like a different guy.

Elinor had e-mailed me the day before to say that now that the interns had conquered their outsides, they wanted to start on the insides. So while waiting for Thom to text me Friday night (he hadn't), I'd planned out Saturday's session, How to Talk to Anyone, complete with three bandannas borrowed from the top of Sabrina's dresser.

I blindfolded Elinor and told her to pretend that Joe was the guy of her dreams, someone she'd never spoken to before. She just happened to run into him and there was no one else around.

"Are you imagining that Joe is the guy of your dreams?" I asked, making sure Elinor's blindfold wasn't loose.

"Yes," she said. She smiled her goofy smile.

"Okay, so, Elinor, you've just run into X, as we'll call him. What do you say?"

"Nothing. I just clam up, break into hives, and then run."

Everyone laughed.

"No, Elinor," I said. "That was the *old* you. The unconfident you. The new Elinor says, 'Hi, I know you from school, right?'"

"But won't that make her look stupid?" Avery asked. "I mean, of course she knows him from school."

"Two reasons," I said. "First: he probably *doesn't* know he knows her from school, so he has to actually think about whether he does. Like when Thom came to the barn that day two years ago, he had no idea who I was or that I went to his school."

"Wait, the first time your boyfriend saw you, he didn't even know he knew you?" Avery asked.

Did she have to harp on the point? "Yeah. Well, no one knew who I was. I was like you said you've been, Avery. An invisible nobody."

"So then you transformed and he wanted to date you?" she asked.

"We're not supposed to be talking about me," I said. "Let's get back to—"

"I would *love* to know how you and Thom got together," Elinor said, peeking out from under the bandanna. "If it's not too personal."

"Yeah, me too," Joe said. "Maybe it'll help me figure out how to approach the girl I want to ask to the Spring Fling."

Fine. "I'll give you the quick version. Right before I went to Rome, Thom came to pick up Sam at the farm. He saw me in the barn feeding one of the calves and asked if he could try it. And so we hung out for a while." I couldn't contain my smile. "And then, out of the blue, he said to me, 'You have the prettiest face.' I almost died."

"And that's when you started going out?" Avery asked.

"He had a girlfriend then." Caro's new bestie, Morgan. "And when I came back from Rome, he didn't even recognize me as the girl he'd met at the farm. When I told him it was me, he was amazed. He asked me out for that night and we've been a couple ever since."

"I love that he liked you before you transformed," Elinor said. "That is so romantic."

"Yeah, but he didn't ask her out *before* she transformed," Avery pointed out.

I glared at her. "Because he had a *girlfriend*."

"I didn't mean that in a bitchy way, I swear," Avery said. "I just wonder if he didn't have a girlfriend if he would have dared ask you out before you were all glam."

"You mean because she wasn't part of his crowd?" Joe asked. "Why would he care? Do guys care about crap like that? I mean, if you like a girl, you like a girl."

"You work like that because you're a good guy," Avery said. "You're not all caught up in who's popular and who's not and what will people think if you ask out a nobody."

I'd asked Thom about that once—whether he would have asked me out that first day at the farm if he hadn't had a girlfriend. He'd said yes. But I remembered not believing it. One of the most popular guys at school asking out a plain farm girl with no friends? No way. I shared that with the interns.

Elinor's eyes widened. "You really don't believe that? But he's your boyfriend."

"Right," Avery said. "So what was he supposed to say? 'No, I wouldn't have asked you out, because even though you're the same girl, you were a loser nobody and I'm Thom Geller and I have a rep to protect'?"

"But I *wasn't* the same girl," I said, now realizing I'd contradicted what I'd said—and believed—earlier. "I was awkward and shy and everything about me was off. I felt uncomfortable in my own skin. That's why I had no friends that first year I moved here. I didn't even really like myself."

They stared at me. I couldn't believe I'd said that. All of that. I felt my cheeks turning red.

"But Thom did like you," Elinor said. "He liked you so much he told you you had the prettiest face. He did like you, you as you were."

Avery bit her lip. "Yeah, that's true."

"See?" Joe said. "Told you guys don't care about that stuff."

Some did, I knew. And I wouldn't ever really know about Thom. I was glad I couldn't know.

"That's really the whole point, isn't it?" Elinor said, pulling a ringlet and letting it spring back.

"Liking yourself. I know this is going to sound conceited, but I've always kind of liked myself. It's just that no one else seems to. Well, except my family and some of the girls from band and mathletes."

"That sounds like a lot of people," Joe said.

"I don't care if anyone likes me," Avery said. "I just want to rule Freeport Academy."

Everyone stopped and stared at her.

And then Elinor said, "Oh, Avery, you are *too* funny!"

But Avery and I locked eyes. And I knew she meant it. She picked up her cute little dog and put him on her lap and began nuzzling his face with her nose. And I thought Caro Alexander was complicated?

I glanced at my watch. Now we only had a half hour left. "Okay, so getting back to starting up a conversation. You say, 'Hi, I know you from school, right?' Or, if you're at school, in the halls or in the caf, you say, 'Hey, you're in my history class, right?' It's a question. He has to respond. You've just initiated a conversation."

"Why does that sound easier than it is?" Joe said.

I smiled. "Try it."

"Can someone else go first?" Joe asked.

"I will!" Elinor said, leaping to her feet. I helped her adjust the bandanna so it covered her eyes again. "Joe, you be the guy I'm crushing on." He stood up again and shoved his hands into his pockets. Elinor clasped and unclasped her hands twice. "Okay, I'm ready." She took a deep breath. "Um, hi—I know you from school, right?"

Joe started blushing. He was definitely going to need a lot of practice at this. "Uh, I think so. Freeport Academy?"

"Yeah," Elinor said, grinning. "I'm a sophomore— well, for three more weeks. You?"

"Yep. Sophomore. So are you going to the Spring Fling dance?"

"I'd like to" was her perfect response.

"Well, in that case, would you like to go with me?" he asked.

She giggled. "Definitely. Yay, I'm going to the Spring Fling with Sam Fray!" she exclaimed.

Oh God. Did Elinor have a crush on Sam too?

She pulled off the blindfold, her face falling a bit when she remembered that it was good old Joe and not really Sam standing next to her.

"You both were great," I said. "Just perfect!"

"So you think I'm ready to try that out on the girl I like?" Joe asked.

"A few more practice runs in the mirror at home and you've got it."

He smiled.

"Oh, I almost forgot," Elinor said, reaching into her backpack. She'd stopped using the bright red one with the little raccoons all over it and switched to a metallic silver one. It was still loud, but in a better way. "Here's the last two hundred we owe you. Sorry we weren't able to give you the full amount up front. Those Cotter twins ran me ragged, but it's been worth every penny and we're still not even done yet. You've really earned the money."

"Ditto," Avery said as she went through her closet.

"Double ditto," Joe said, nodding at me.

"I think that's 'tritto,'" Elinor said, furrowing her brow. "Avery, can I look up 'tritto' on your computer?" At Avery's okay, Elinor started searching. "Yup, definitely 'tritto.'"

Only Elinor.

"Well, then, tritto," Joe said.

I slid the envelope into my messenger bag. I had it all now. The four hundred dollars that would take me to California. So why wasn't *I* asking Avery to borrow her computer so I could book my ticket right then? Maybe it was enough to know I had the money.

I glanced at Elinor. She was standing in front of the floor-length mirror on the outside of Avery's closet, mouthing her new lines. She looked so excited, so happy. My stomach sank. If she really had a crush on Sam, she was about to get her heart smashed.

• • •

After our class, Elinor and I walked to Main Street so she could sign up for the Lobster Claw Teen Queen Pageant. Now that she had almost two weeks of classes under her belt, Elinor finally felt secure in registering. She clutched the ad she'd cut out from the paper.

LOBSTER CLAW TEEN QUEEN PAGEANT AND PARADE!

Are you the next Lobster Claw Teen Queen? Entrants must be between the ages of 13 and 17 and will be judged on poise, talent, and an essay to be read aloud on what it means to be a teen today. 500 words minimum, 750 maximum. The winner will ride in a float down Main Street during the Lobster Claw Festival parade, see her winning essay printed in the Freeport Times, and receive a grand prize of $1,000!

"I forgot about the talent component," I said. "What's your specialty?"

"Either a modern-dance routine, reciting a passage from one of my favorite Shakespeare plays, or possibly a brief clarinet piece."

"You can do all that? And *well*?"

She bit her lip. "I can sing okay too, but I can't sing and dance at the same time. I totally lose my breath. Anyway, Caro sings. I have a better chance of placing if I do something different."

Caro always sang. She had an amazing voice, rock meets opera. She always sang some old rhythm-and-blues song that stopped people in their tracks.

On the lawn of the town hall, a woman sat behind a table with a clipboard and a stack of pink packets. The line to register wasn't that long. There were maybe seven or eight people, girls and their mothers. Caro and her mom were near the front of the line when we arrived. I waved at Caro and she shot me a look of pure disgust. I knew what it meant: *Why are you in public with that Not?*

I was getting sick of the dirty looks. Sick of being told—or very loudly not told—who I could talk to or associate with.

After Caro registered, she and her mom started walking toward the parking lot, but as her mom got into the car, Caro waved me over.

"I'll be right back, Elinor," I said.

Caro's hands were on her hips. "What the hell do you think you're doing?"

"I'm just offering moral support," I said. "It's her first time signing up."

"In my clothes," she said. "I want them back, Madeline. I've had it."

"Caro, she's just borrowing them from me."

"No, *you're* just borrowing them from *me*. I didn't say she could wear my stuff. And didn't we just have this conversation?"

"Caro, come on. We're talking about Elinor Espinoza. Do you really care?"

"I don't care about Smelinor Whateveroza, Madeline. I just don't want my clothes on the backs of these . . . people."

Bitch. Bitch. Bitch. "Fine. I'll tell her I need them back."

"Good."

She crossed her arms over her chest and glanced at the line. "And another thing. I can't believe you're actually helping another candidate, Madeline."

I laughed. "Right. Like you have competition, Caro."

"Did I use the word 'competition'? And anyway, that's not the point. Anyone who enters the pageant is running against me. You know all my secrets—my beauty regimen, my best talents. You'll use all that to help that loser."

"Caro—"

"I'm disappointed," she said in her mother's tone, then got into her car.

Oh God. I watched the Mercedes drive away and felt my stomach turn over and twist. How had all this happened? How had I gone from wanting to see my boyfriend and go to my dad's wedding to not getting along with my best friend? To being shut out? Now I was a traitor for helping Elinor?

"Is she mad at you?" Elinor asked when I joined her in line. "She looked upset."

I looked at Elinor. This pageant meant so much to her. For Caro, it was just another trophy. I did want Elinor to do well in the pageant, because . . .

I liked her.

Yeah, I liked her. I liked her and I liked Joe and I even liked Avery, even though she had some Caro-like traits.

"Well, I'm helping her competition, so . . ."

Elinor laughed. "That's hilarious. Like I even register on her radar!"

That was interesting, actually. That Elinor did register. Was Caro Alexander really that insecure?

"I guess it's the principle," I said. But I knew that Caro seriously couldn't be worried about Elinor. This was more about me. Controlling me, wielding her power.

"She's Caro Alexander. She's still going to win," Elinor said. "I just want to place. No, I don't even care about placing. I just want to enter and feel like I *could* place. I just want my stepmother off my back."

"I know. Don't worry about it."

"Okay," she said. "If you're sure. I don't want to cause trouble for you."

I smiled. "Honestly, don't worry about it."

"You know what I *am* worrying about? My dress

141

for the pageant. I don't have anything, and if I ask my stepmother to buy me a new dress, she'll drag me to her favorite store and I'll end up with something she chose, because she's the one with the wallet. That's pretty much why I never have any new clothes. My mom can't afford it, and my stepmother has total mother-of-the-bride taste."

"I didn't know you really cared so much about clothes."

"I don't, really, but . . . there's this dress I wish I could wear in the pageant, but it costs a fortune and I'd never buy something I could only wear once. I mean, it's not like I need the fancy dress of my dreams for school dances. Though a guy I sort of like has kind of been paying attention to me." She couldn't contain the glow under her shyness and started twirling around. "He's really cute. Omigod, wouldn't it be amazing if he asked me to the Spring Fling? Madeline, for the first time in my life, I really think something I want might actually come true."

I leaned over and hugged her and she squeezed me back.

"So where'd you see this amazing dress? At the mall?"

She shook her head. "No, I saw it in Retro Girl, the vintage-clothing store down by the bead shop. It's this incredible hot pink and has these layers of chiffon. And it has this gorgeous matching flower at the bottom of the strap. It's so me and I even tried it on. But it would be silly to buy it for a one-hour event that I'm not even going to win. Though the pictures would be cool to have. Anyway, I'll just wear something I have and imagine I'm in that dress. That's something Anne of *Anne of Green Gables* would do. The importance of imagination and all."

I wasn't sure what she was talking about, but I nodded anyway. "Yeah, I'll just imagine I'm wearing that amazing dress," she continued. "Oh, and, Madeline, I totally don't expect you to cheer for me or anything. I know you'll be cheering for Caro. She's your best friend."

Right. My best friend.

I called Caro that night. "So has Sam asked you out?"

"God, Madeline," she said. "Don't you think I'd tell you if he had? You don't need to rub it in my face that he hasn't. It's embarrassing *enough*."

Whoa. "Caro, I was just ask—"

"Whatever. Let's just change the subject. I assume you told the frizz freak you're not helping her with the Lobster Claw Teen Queen Pageant."

I closed my eyes and flopped down on my bed.

"Caro, she's paying my airfare to see Thom and to attend my dad's wedding. I *have* to help her."

"Right. You have to help her against a friend."

"Caro, it's ridiculous—"

"Oh, so now I'm ridiculous?" she asked.

"Caro, come on,"

"No, *you* come on, Madeline. You're being really weird and everyone is talking about it. Let's face it. Thom is gone. And, look, I'm not saying we're not real friends, because we are, but Thom is the reason we took you into our group in the first place. That's not mean, it's just a *fact*. You and Thom were a package deal. If I were you, I'd hook up with James or Reid, and fast. And I'd lose the farm freaks."

I almost dropped the phone. That creepy feeling, the one that twisted my stomach into knots and gave me headaches and made me feel crazy, the one that had started when Caro had begun acting weird before Thom even left, was back. With a vengeance. *Real friends.* What did *that* mean?

Okay, just take a breath, Madeline. I closed my eyes and breathed in and out.

"I'll assume your silence means what I said is slowly sinking in," Caro said.

"So we're not real friends or we are, Caro? Which is it?"

"I'm just saying, Madeline."

"Well, I can't lose the *farm freaks*. They're paying my way to California. You know that."

"Madeline, have you even heard from Thom lately? He used to call and text every hour. Now you're lucky if he texts you once a day to say he's so busy. And what do you think he's busy with? His new friends? A new girlfriend. Wake up and smell the cow crap, Madeline."

Tears pricked the backs of my eyes. "Thanks, Caro. Thanks a lot."

She was silent for a moment. "Sweetie, I'm telling you the truth because I'm your best friend. Do you really want me to lie to your face and tell you what you want to hear?"

"Do you really think Thom has dumped me without telling me?"

"Ninety-nine percent chance of yes," she said. "I'd wear something sexy tomorrow and flirt with James. You can borrow my sparkly pink T-shirt that you like."

"I don't know about anything," I said. "I'm gonna go, okay?"

"Okay. And, Mads, don't worry so much. We have your back." *Click.*

I stared at the ceiling. Was I delusional about Thom? Was he making out with some girl right then? Was California just going to be a huge waste of money?

145

I picked up Caro's present—the hearted-up yearbook—and flipped to Reid's and James's pages. They *were* very cute. If I just picked one of them and started hanging out with him, maybe I'd like him. And my life could go back to normal. I'd be part of an It Couple. I'd have my place in my world again. Everything would be okay. And I could still see Thom in California, because I'd be there anyway for my dad's wedding.

I glanced at James's cute face. He did absolutely nothing for me. I didn't want to know what music he liked or if he thought Yum's or Pizza Palace was more fun to hang out in. I didn't want to kiss him.

And Thom? Thom was beginning to feel like a memory.

How had that happened so fast?

I flipped to his photo and I smiled. Those green eyes stared into mine and I had to admit I still missed him, but not with the intensity I had at first. Maybe because so much had happened.

On the left side of the page were the "F"s, including Sam Fray. My gaze shifted to his photo, and *his* was the one I couldn't take my eyes off.

Chapter 14

I called Thom. Got his voice mail. Texted him: *Really need to talk.* Then I waited almost an hour. Nothing. Maybe if we did talk, we could settle something. Were we still a couple?

I thought about calling Fergie, but she tended to get very nervous about talking about Caro behind her back. Which was smart.

You know, Madeline, if you ever need to talk . . .

I changed my shoes and headed out to the small barn, but Sam wasn't there. He didn't usually stay that late, but he'd volunteered to help Mac and the farmhand move the cows to the far pasture. I headed that way, up the hilly path that wound its way through almost fifty acres of land. For a moment I stopped and stared at the clear blue sky, at a fluffy white cloud in the shape of Mickey Mouse's head, and then took a deep breath. I kept heading up until I saw the herd of cows, and then there was Sam, sitting on a rock and writing something in a notebook, his back against a tree.

"Hey," I said.

"Mac or your mom need me?" he asked, taking off his sunglasses and squinting up at me, those brown eyes so warm and intense at the same time.

"Nope," I said. "I do, actually." For Joe, I made a mental note of what Sam was wearing—faded army green cargo pants and a black T-shirt, a dark brown leather band around his wrist. I couldn't see Joe wearing a leather bracelet.

He closed the notebook and patted the rock next to him. "What's up?"

"Oh, just everything is completely falling apart," I said. "My friends are mad at me. My boyfriend—who I'm not sure is still my boyfriend—is three thousand miles away. My dad is getting married to a woman I've never met, and doesn't seem to care if I go to the wedding or not."

"Ah, that *is* everything," he said, and for a second, I found it hard to look away. His face was so . . . . nice to look at, and his eyes were so warm, and his lips looked so kissable—

I did want to kiss him. Right then.

I forced myself to stare out at the pasture, at the six or seven cows standing around, some grazing, some doing absolutely nothing. "I—I'm just trying to do what feels right to me," I said. "But it's not necessarily right to other people."

"That's usually the case," he said. "People feel differently about things. You can't please everyone, right?"

"Yeah, but what about alliances?" I asked. "Someone is asking me to be loyal. But in this specific case, it just doesn't make sense. It shouldn't be about loyalty. Or maybe it should—I don't know."

"I know all about loyalty," he said. "Especially to a friend. But there are circumstances when being loyal is being stupid."

"Like when?"

"Like when you really like a girl and want to ask her out, but you're not sure if she's really into her boyfriend, who used to be your best friend, but he's three thousand miles away. And you don't want to be a jerk by asking her out, but you don't want to be stupid and not ask her out when at least five of your friends are seriously lusting after her."

Butterflies started flying around in my stomach and I tried to suppress the warm, happy feeling—and my smile. But I couldn't.

Until I had to say something. "Sam, I—" What? What was I supposed to say? *I like you too, but I can't, because Caro wants you and she has dibs and she's my sort-of best friend, but she's really not anymore, and if I go for you, I'm dead. Dead at school. None of my friends will talk to me. It'll be worse than it was in eighth grade, because I won't be invisible—I'll be an outcast.*

But I want to go for you. So, so much.

I'd just realized something. This wasn't about loyalty at all. It was about *fear.*

I suddenly knew why he had fooled around with Caro. To get me out of his system. He knew she liked him, and he knew I couldn't say yes to him because of that. So he'd decided to go for it. Caro was beautiful and hard to resist and he'd gone for it because she'd made it so easy by putting his hands on her chest. But he'd avoided her since.

He took my hand and held for it a moment. "I probably just made things even worse for you, didn't I?"

I smiled. "Yeah, you did."

"So what now?" he asked, those brown eyes looking right into mine. He didn't let my hand go. And I didn't pull it away.

"Now I need to figure some stuff out," I told him.

"You know where to find me."

I decided to feign being sick when Caro called to tell me what time we were meeting at Coffee Connection. The five of us, and sometimes some other girls and some of the guys, met at Coffee Connection every Sunday morning around eleven.

But it was ten-thirty and she hadn't called yet. I reached for my phone to make sure I hadn't turned it off the night before. I'd fallen asleep giving Joe instructions on purchasing green cargo pants and a black T-shirt.

Nope. Phone was on. No calls. No texts.

Now that she was back to shutting me out after being all nicey-nicey—sort of—on the phone the other day, that funny feeling slid its way into my stomach. They were all at Coffee Connection without me.

I was an outcast and I hadn't even crossed a line yet.

And I didn't like the feeling at all.

I got up and took a fast shower, put on an outfit that made me feel all girl-powery, and asked my mom for a ride to Coffee Connection.

There they were. The four of them—Caro, Fergie, Selena, and Annie—sat at a large square table in the back, one second deep in conversation, the next laughing.

To seem unfazed, I got a latte and a chocolate chip muffin, then took a deep breath and headed to the table with my tray. No one paid the slightest bit of attention to me.

"Hey," I said, trying to hide how unsure I felt. "No one called me."

"Oh," Caro said, picking up her latte and taking a long sip.

Oh? That was it?

"We thought you'd be giving worthless beauty tips to rejects," Fergie said, and Annie burst into laughter.

Selena put her scone down. "All of a sudden you're, like, hanging out with these loser misfits all the time. Letting them wear Caro's clothes. And you're actually walking around town with Smelinor and helping her enter Caro's pageant?"

My blood started boiling. "You all *know* what I'm doing. They paid me four hundred dollars to transform them from Nots into normal people. Am I not supposed to do my job?"

"Just don't do it at my expense," Caro said.

Fergie nodded. "Yeah, Madeline. And who is this Avery chick strutting around in the little black minidress I gave you for your birthday last year? She suddenly thinks she's all that. And she's not."

Actually, she sort of was. Enough to threaten this tough table.

"So not," Caro agreed. "And by the way, I want you to do something for me."

I waited. Nervously.

She took another slow sip of her latte, then looked at me. "Sam's been scarce these past few days. But three times a week, he's at your farm. I want you to find out—surreptitiously, of course— what he likes in a girl. His last three girlfriends have all been wildly different, so I can't figure out what it is I'm doing wrong, where I'm going wrong in hooking him. I want him to be my boyfriend by next weekend at the latest. You can get the info out of him, right, Madeline?"

I know what he likes in a girl—me! I wanted to scream. And I wanted to just plain scream. This was insane. What was I supposed to do? Pretend I talked to him and tell Caro lies? How was I supposed to get out of this?

"Wait, are you planning to change into what he likes?" Fergie asked Caro. "I mean, if he likes girls who are arty or skater rats or do-gooding candy stripers, are you going to do that kind of stuff just to hook him?"

"I'd do whatever it takes. I just need to hook him," Caro said. "Once he gets to know me better, he'll be totally into me."

"Why?" Fergie asked two beats later. "I mean, if he's into artsy girls with purple tips at the ends of their hair, like that freak Alanna whatever-her-last-name-is, are you going to get purple tips and turn

153

Goth or something? How will he fall in love with you if you're not really like that?"

"I don't have to get all Goth," Caro said. "I just have to study up on whatever he's into, so I can talk about it, act like I'm into it. If that's how I need to get his attention, so be it."

"Sort of like what Madeline is doing with the Nots," Fergie said.

Caro turned a killer stare on Fergie. "Don't ever compare me to those losers, Fergie. I'm just trying to strategize on getting a guy who's playing hard to get."

I closed my eyes and wanted to slink away. Far, far away.

Caro fixed her stare on me. "So you'll find out what he's into?"

I bit my lip and nodded.

This sucked. Everything sucked. Everything but the way Sam had made me feel in the pasture. Everything but the way just the thought of him started that warm, goopy feeling.

If you say yes to Sam, you're over, I reminded myself. *You're an outcast among the popular girls at Freeport Academy. And no trip to Rome will solve that.*

Ah, but a trip to California could solve a lot. No, not because of Thom. We were over. I didn't need him to confirm what was glaringly obvious. And I liked someone else, anyway. Someone I couldn't have unless I wanted to ruin my life. And not having Sam because of Caro would eat away at me and I'd hate her.

So, yeah, California was looking even sunnier than before. It would be running away, but it would be a fresh start. I could just start over.

Wherever you go, there you are, I heard Sabrina say in my head.

Chapter 15

I did what I always did when I was confused and upset and scared: I headed for the calves' barn. Hermione was sleeping on the hay, so I sat down on the tiny stool in Weasley's corral and petted his black and white spotted back. He nudged his pink nose on my arm, hoping for an apple slice. But all I had was me.

"Hey, hon," my mom called as she passed by carrying two buckets of feed. "How's everything?"

Everything was the worst it could possibly be.

If she'd just kept on going, if she'd only thrown me that question the way people always did, and kept walking without expecting an answer, I might not have said anything. But she put down the buckets and leaned against the wooden gate in front of Weasley's pen.

"Mom, I'm just going to ask you this outright, and it doesn't mean I want to do it, just that I've been sort of thinking about it, okay?"

"Okay," she said, concern in her blue eyes.

"I've been thinking about asking Dad if I could live with him for the summer and, um, actually finish out high school in California."

Her eyes widened. Not a hurt look. Not an angry look. Just surprised. "Are you that unhappy here?" She opened the gate, came into the pen, and sat down right on the hay beside me.

I didn't say anything, couldn't say anything. All of a sudden, tears flooded my eyes and I started crying like a five-year-old.

My mom reached over and pulled me into a hug. "Sweetheart, I know you and Thom have been a couple for a long time, but you can't pin your hopes and a life-changing move on a boy. You'd have to want to move to California because you miss your father and because you hate it here."

I sniffed. "I do miss Dad, sort of. But I don't hate it here. Ugh, I don't know anything anymore. I thought moving to California would solve my problems with my friends and I could keep Thom or maybe meet someone else, and I could have Dad back, you know, the way it used to be between us when he actually seemed to care about us, but

I don't want to leave you and Mac. Or even Sabrina. Or Hermione."

She tightened her hug and held me for a minute. "Sweetie, if you want to live with your dad, that's a conversation you'll need to have with him. I'll support you no matter what. I want you here, but I'll support you."

My mom rocked. She totally, totally rocked. "I love you," I whispered, and let her hug me like I was a little kid.

"I know. And I love you too."

Weasley started chewing on the sleeve of my hoodie, so I jumped up.

"Come on, I'll make you your favorite lunch," my mom said, and we headed out of the barn together.

I still had no idea what I was going to do, but I felt tons better.

When I saw Sam raking out stalls alone in the cows' barn, I stood by the huge wooden door and watched him, watched the way his muscles moved under his T-shirt. He was softly singing, but I couldn't make out the words.

He glanced over and saw me. His smile lit up the dark barn. "Hey," he said.

"Hey." I walked in, turned over a big metal

bucket, and sat down on it. I'd figured out a way to ask Sam about his type and relay that info to Caro without lying or bringing myself into the equation. I had no idea what would happen. Caro would become more like me to hook Sam? And then he'd suddenly like her? It didn't work like that. At least, I hoped it didn't. I was now helping Caro get the guy I wanted so that she wouldn't dump me as a friend and make my life a living misery at school. Yeah, that made a lot of sense.

"So, Sam, about this girl you like—you know, the one you haven't been sure is single—why do you like her, anyway?"

He stopped raking and looked right at me. "She's beautiful. But so are a lot of girls at Freeport Academy. This one is . . . special."

My heart swelled. "Why?" I asked.

"Can't really put my finger on it. She's nice, and I like that, but it's more than that."

This wasn't helping—which was good, because vague wouldn't help Caro, but it still counted as information. I'd done my job.

"Are you asking because you're trying to make a decision?"

I nodded.

"Okay," he said, and went back to raking. I loved that he didn't press me. He just let it be.

"So how's the image thing going with the other interns?" he asked.

"You heard about that?"

"I heard Caro and Fergie telling Tate and Ceej about it at lunch. And Elinor and Joe were talking about it the other day."

"I'm just trying to help them be happier," I said. "I'm not sure if anything I'm doing will change anything."

"It already has," he said. "Joe looks like a completely different guy. And he acts differently too. He's not as shy as he used to be. He actually carries on a conversation with me now. Before, he couldn't get three words out."

I smiled. "That's great."

"Sam?" Mac called. "Got a sec? I need help bringing pen four to the grazing pasture."

"Coming," he called out. "Talk to you later," he said to me, those brown eyes lingering on mine.

Caro called that night.

"Well, did you find out anything?"

Okay. Just tell her a cleaned-up version of the truth. "Well, he said he likes someone who he's not so sure is single, so I asked him why he liked this girl, and—"

160

"Meaning *you*, Madeline?"

"Me?" I repeated, playing dumb.

"Madeline, he stares at you all the time. The only reason he hasn't asked you out is because you talk about your long-lost boyfriend all day. It's clear he likes you."

"If he really liked me, Caro, he'd have asked me out. Come on. Thom's long gone. And I haven't heard from him in a while. I'm sure Sam knows that. They probably still talk or text or whatever."

Dead silence. And then, "So why *does* Sam like you so much?"

"Caro, he didn't come right out and say he was talking about me. He *could* be talking about anyone. But he did say the girl he likes is nice, but that's not the entire reason he likes her. He said he can't put his finger on it."

"So I have to be *nicer* to hook Sam," she said. I could see her rolling her eyes. "I hate nice."

I laughed. That was actually funny. "You could try, you know."

Not that I wanted her to try. I wanted her to go on being mean so that Sam wouldn't like her. But I wanted her to turn nice so we could be friends again.

Either way, she wasn't going to end up my friend. That much I knew.

"God, I hate this," she said. "Love sucks."

"Tell me about it."

"Well, thanks for trying, Madeline. I appreciate it."

"No problem, Caro."

"See you tomorrow morning," she said. And just like that, things were "okay" again.

Chapter 16

Sam was having a party on Saturday night. I didn't even have to ask if I could invite the interns. He'd invited them himself. He'd even invited Sabrina and her even weirder friend, the one who also wore overalls all the time.

Yes, Sam was nice.

And good thing, because the party would provide the perfect opportunity for the new-and-improved interns to test themselves out. *Everyone* showed up at Sam's parties, all the different cliques—the Gothy art rats, the crunchers, the jocks, the stoners, the wannabes, and the Mosts, guys and girls. And Caro Alexander rarely showed up at a party unless it was her own or a junior or senior Most's.

The interns and I spent our class hour at Elinor's house, deciding on clothes and discussing important party points, such as what to do when you first walked in, where to stand, what to say. Avery was giving Elinor and Joe as much advice as I was. And she'd earned the right. She looked like a page out of *InStyle*.

"Let's practice," Elinor said, grabbing Joe's arm. Elinor pulled him out into the hallway, shut the door, then knocked.

"Actually, you don't have to knock," I called out. "The front door will be open. Just open the screen door and walk right in."

"Really?" Elinor shouted through the door. "Isn't that rude?"

"Not at this kind of party," I said. I walked over to the door and opened it. "Pretend there's a screen door and that you can see a party going on inside. People might be on the front lawn, too, but that's unusual. Mostly everyone will be inside or out back."

"Oh God, I'm so nervous," Elinor said. "No, I mean for real. Right now. I'm nervous about even walking through the fake door into the fake party. How am I going to actually walk into Sam Fray's house full of everyone at school who makes fun of me on a daily basis?"

"Has anyone made fun of you lately?" Avery asked.

Elinor bit her lip. "Actually, no. Well, there are

always a few meanies in gym. They still call me dork when I miss the volleyball, that kind of thing."

"There are always going to be mean people," I said. "You just have to ignore them and not let them get to you."

"Easier said than done," Elinor said. "Even when you're *improved*."

That was definitely true. Caro and Fergie got to me.

"Just remember this," I said. "Sam invited you all. You are his friends. His coworkers. His classmates. You were invited. You belong there like anyone else at that party. And if you walk in like you know that, you'll be fine. Own it."

"She's absolutely right," Avery said. "That's how I feel now. It took a while, but I really feel that way."

Elinor and Joe did some kind of corny hand bump, then went back into the hallway. Elinor pulled open the imaginary screen door.

"Hi, I'm Elinor!" she said to the armoire. "Great party." Silence. "Great party, huh?" she said again.

"Is she supposed to say that?" Joe asked.

"How about this?" I said, stepping into the hall. I pulled open the imaginary screen door as Elinor had. "Hey," I said to the armoire with a quick, warm smile. Then I pretended to weave my way around some people. "Hi. Oh, hi, how are you? Warm smile all around. Eye contact, but not longer than 1.5 seconds." I stopped and turned to the interns. "Okay, now I'm thinking, *Oooh, that guy is really cute. I have to think of something to say to him to get into a conversation.* Hi, do you know where the kitchen is? I'm sooo thirsty." I turned my voice deep. "It's right over there," I said, pointing. "I'll go with you. I'm thirsty too." I changed my voice back to my own. "I'm Elinor." I changed my voice again. "Jesse. You're in my history class, right?" I took a bow, then said, "That's how it's done."

"That was so good," Elinor said. "I think I can do that."

"Me too," Joe said. "That's just normal conversation."

"That's the point," I said. "You don't have to be all nervous and repeat things or try to come up with something brilliant or cutesy to say. You be yourself."

Joe wanted to go next and had to start over a couple of times, but by the fourth time, he did great. He even "talked" to the captain of the junior varsity football team, Ceej, who intimidated him. And then he asked out his dream girl. And she said yes.

"I'll bet she does say yes," Elinor said. "That was awesome."

"I'm really proud of you guys," I said. "You're going to do great." I looked at my watch. "I have to go." My mom was dropping me at Fergie's to get ready for the party, and Caro's housekeeper was going to pick us up and drive us. "So we're clear, right?" I asked. "No one wears any of the stuff I let you borrow, or Caro and Fergie will freak, okay?"

"I promise I won't," Joe joked.

Joe had come a long way, from being afraid to say anything to cracking jokes—cute jokes—and really showing who he was: a nice, funny guy.

Avery glanced up from where she sat on the floor in front of the mirror on Elinor's closet door. She was trying on lipsticks. "What is the big deal if we wear their cast-off clothes that they gave away? They're such *bitches*."

Everyone stopped and stared at her, then me.

"It's okay," I said. "They *are* bitches. But they can be really nice, too." Not lately, though. I glanced at Avery but couldn't read her expression.

"What's Caro Alexander actually like?" Elinor asked. "I just sort of think of her as like a movie star or pop star."

"She's just a *girl*," Avery said, moving around pieces of her hair as she looked in the mirror. "She's done absolutely nothing to earn star status. She's not an actress or a singer or the winner of the Pulitzer prize. She's just a girl."

"She's not just a girl," Elinor said. "She's Most *Beautiful*. She's Most Everything."

"Well, she didn't do anything to earn that," Avery countered. "She's beautiful and rich. So what? Madeline is self-made," she added, glancing at me. "That's why I respect her. She went from nothing to something."

Whoa, lighten up, I wanted to say, but she was so dead serious I let it go.

"You're so lucky you don't have to get all done up," Fergie said to me. "When you like someone, and he's going to be at the party, you have to spend hours on just your *skin*. I started getting ready for this party on Thursday. You're almost lucky you're 'involved' in a long-distance relationship. Totally takes the pressure off."

She made big honking air quotes around the "involved."

Whatever. She wasn't baiting me. I had no idea how I felt about anything, and there was no way Mary Margaret Ferragamo was going to get me all upset tonight.

We were in Fergie's bedroom. She'd changed her outfit three times. The first time because Caro was wearing all white, and Fergie had originally decided on a white sleeveless little dress. The outfit she'd planned, complete with accessories, had had to go because of Caro's white skirt, which Caro had decided on two seconds before leaving her house—after Fergie had called to confirm their outfits twice that day.

"Omigod, Caro," Fergie complained, frowning at outfit number four: a very cute flouncy tank top and her new gazillion-dollar jeans and very high-heeled sandals. "Can I just wear my white dress? Nothing feels right now because I was so set on the white dress."

"Fergie, live up to your status," Caro called from the bathroom, where she was putting the finishing touches on her makeup. "You should be able to change your outfit at a moment's notice and look amazing. You're just having a mental block. Get past it."

Fergie rolled her eyes at me in the mirror.

I smiled. "Fergie, what you're wearing is totally hot."

Caro poked her head out to check out Fergie. "Very. You'll have me to thank when you and Tate are voted Class Couple in less than two weeks."

Fergie's gaze drifted over to me. "You're okay with that, right, Madeline? I mean, it's not like you and Thom are *really* even together anymore. I know you're hanging on to him, but still."

I wanted to punch her. Seriously.

"And, honey," Caro said in her fake, syrupy voice, "I'm worried about you actually hooking someone like James or Reid. I mean, you're spending *way* too much time with the freaks. People are noticing. And, I hate to tell you this, Madeline, but who knows what's rubbing off on you?"

"Meaning?" I asked.

"Meaning, when you spend a lot of time with freaks, there's the danger of turning into one yourself."

"That's actually true," Fergie said. "Cliques look alike. The art idiots in their stupid ripped patterned tights and fake tattoos, the nerds in their nerd wear, the stoners in their totally heinous tie-dye."

"Could we *please* talk about something else?" I said. "You know they're paying me. It's my ticket to my dad's wedding."

Caro laughed. "Ooh, we've made progress. Last week it was your ticket to see Thom."

I was hating Caro more by the second.

"Okay, Madeline, time to dress you," Fergie interrupted. She eyed Caro, then said, "Okay, so no white. I have the perfect outfit for you." She handed me something folded over a hanger. "Try it on."

I wasn't so sure about the "perfect outfit." It was a sparkly lavender—but it appeared to be a jumpsuit, made out of some kind of jersey, with a lot of material around the waist and a low-slung tie belt at the hips. I couldn't even find the neck opening.

"Wait a minute. Is this a jumpsuit?" I asked. "It has legs, but it's one piece."

Fergie held it up against me. "My mom bought it in Prague last year. Hot new designer—all the rage. I begged for it, but I haven't even had a chance to wear it. You're the first."

Well, I did like the color. And it was from Prague; that sounded cool. "I'll try it on."

Trying it on took like twenty minutes. I couldn't figure out how to adjust the material at the waist or how to get the belt to lie just right. I left the bathroom. "Fergie, I think I need your help. But I'm not so sure this is right for me anyway. It's so . . . baggy."

"It's not baggy," she said. "It's *voluminous*. And totally haute couture. I was reading Italian *Vogue* this morning, and 'voluminous' is the word for the fall season from the runways. I'd think you'd keep up with what was coming out of the fashion houses in Milan."

"I love it," Caro said, tilting her head to look me up and down. "You look amazing, Madeline. Really elegant."

I glanced in the floor-to-ceiling mirror, which took up an entire wall of Fergie's bedroom. I didn't look amazing. I didn't look elegant. I looked *awful*.

Oh.

Was that their point? To make me look awful for the party? So that Sam would lose interest in me?

"Sorry, Fergie." I pulled the jumpsuit off my body. "I'll just stick to what I came in wearing." Which was a perfectly good outfit for a summer party. A simple ice-blue cotton tank dress with a cool silver necklace I'd bought at an art fair and my silver wedge sandals.

"If you want to look boring," Caro told me. "But like Fergie said, it really doesn't matter. You're hanging your hopes on a guy who's three thousand miles away, and you're *not* interested in two very hot guys who are interested in you—and who will be at the party. You could wear a garbage bag and it wouldn't make a diff. I don't even know why you're bothering to go at all."

But I did.

Chapter 17

Sam's party was packed. When we walked through the front door, the crowd immediately parted. There was the usual "Hi! I love your hair, your dress, your earrings, your shoes, that is the cutest necklace, your hair is so pretty." I could swear that a girl even said, "Can I touch you?"

I smiled and said hi; Caro and Fergie, chins slightly raised, moved forward, their gazes resting on no one.

The guys were outside on the deck. The moment we pulled open the sliding glass door, the girls who were on the deck scattered like mice. Ceej tried to spin Fergie around in a weird hello, but she said, "Don't even think about touching me ever again. Have you forgotten we're very over?"

And then there was Sam, leaning against the

deck railing, wearing faded gray cargos and a white T-shirt and drinking a lemon-lime Gatorade.

He was so cute. I couldn't take my eyes off him. And not just because of how good-looking he was, but because of how nice he was. How easy to talk to. He did his own thing, from interning at the farm—which everyone found cool when *he* did it, just not when uncool people did it, which made no sense—to inviting all kinds of people to his party. The popular and the not so popular. Sam was just himself and totally comfortable with that.

I wished I could be that way.

Before I could even say hi, Caro walked over and draped herself across him.

"Hi," she said, giving him a kiss on the cheek and pressing her body against his.

"Hi," he said. He looked at me for a long moment. "Hi, Madeline. Fergie," he added. Then he moved slightly away from Caro and took a sip of his drink. Caro's face fell, but she recovered in a second.

"Hey, James," she called behind me. "Come say hi."

James and Reid and two other guys crowded around us. "Madeline was just asking if you were here yet, James."

Sam glanced at me. I shot Caro a look. I hadn't said a word to her about James.

James smiled at me, then stared at my chest. "I'll

go get us something to drink," he said, and then left.

Ugh. He was making it very easy for me to justify avoiding him for the rest of the party. *But nice try, Caro.* He walked back inside the house and I let out the breath I hadn't even known I was holding.

"Sam, get *me* something ice cold to drink, will you, sweetie?" Caro said to him. "Feel free to add something naughty to it," she whispered loudly in his ear. And while he headed inside, she draped herself against the railing.

"Where's Tate?" Caro asked for Fergie, whose eyes were darting all over the lawn for him.

"Don't know," Ceej said. "He hasn't shown up yet."

A group of giggling girls started to come out onto the deck, but when they saw us, they retreated inside. I wanted to follow them, escape with them.

"Omigod, it is so buggy out here," Caro said. "Let's go take over the sofas. And someone *change* this CD. I hate this chick's voice."

I swatted a mosquito as we headed inside. The moment I heard the sliding glass door click behind me, the front door opened and in walked Elinor and Joe.

"Oh, look, it's your little farm freaks," Caro whispered, just in case Sam was in earshot.

I smiled and waved at them, and they waved back. Elinor waved too excitedly, but she didn't jump. That was something.

"They actually look half human," Fergie said. "And they're not even wearing our clothes. Wow, Madeline, you have worked wonders."

That was a serious compliment, coming from Fergie. "Thanks. I'm gonna go get some pretzels or something. Be right back."

As if I could eat anything. I just wanted to say hi to Elinor and Joe and ask where Avery was. I hoped she hadn't chickened out of coming.

I wove my way through the crowd, past a couple making out in the same spot, same position as when we'd arrived, past a bunch of guys who had their shirts off and were asking a group of girls who had the best abs, past person after person I didn't even recognize who smiled at me and said hi.

James shoved a cup of something brown with an ice cube floating in it at me. Girls around us were checking him out. They could have him.

"Um, thanks," I said, taking the cup. "I see someone I have to go say hi to. Catch up with you later, okay?"

"Hope so," he said, and turned to talk to the busty girl behind me.

I finally made my way to Elinor and Joe by the food table. "Hey, guys." There were bowls of just about every kind of snack, from M&M'S to potato chips and several different dips. There were even platters of crudités, the only things Caro, Fergie, Selena, and Annie would eat. "You look great."

Joe and Elinor were both looking around, obviously excited to be there.

"Wow, so this is a party," Joe said. "Awesome."

"So cool," Elinor whispered.

Then Joe stood a little straighter. "There she is."

I glanced around, trying to follow his gaze, but the party was so crowded that he could be talking about the grandfather clock near the fireplace. That was the general direction he was looking in.

Everyone was there. There must have been a hundred people. I spotted Sabrina and her weird friend by another table laden with Mexican fiesta food—various colorful bowls of beans and salsa and tortilla chips. She'd just dropped a Frito piled with what looked like hummus right onto her shirt. Her response? Bursting into laughter and reaching for a napkin. Fergie or Caro would have screamed and gone home to change. Not that Fergie or Caro would eat a single chip in the first place.

I waved at Sabrina, but I didn't think she saw me. At least she wasn't wearing overalls. For a moment, as I watched my sister, I couldn't imagine moving to California and not living with her and our mom and Mac. I could imagine not living on the farm, but I couldn't imagine not living with my family. Sabrina and me on opposite coasts? She'd always been right there—weirdly right there, annoyingly right there, but *there*.

"Okay, go enjoy yourselves," I said.

They stayed rooted in their spots.

"Go," I told them. "You'll be fine. Just remember what you practiced. Keep it short and simple. A passing hi. A 'You're in my English class, right?' You can do it."

They nodded and Elinor led the way farther into the crowd. I headed back to where my friends were sitting.

"Where is Sam?" Caro muttered.

"He probably got stuck talking to somebody," Fergie said. "You've got all night. *All* night," she repeated, sending Caro a devilish smile.

Caro smiled back and relaxed.

Suddenly, the thought of Caro and Sam together, *that way,* made me want to vomit.

Annie and Selena and half the cheerleading squad arrived and squeezed into the other chairs and sofas, and even onto the floor. Annie was telling us a story about something that had happened in her gym class on Friday and everyone was cracking up. For a moment, I let myself be swept up by it all, even though I couldn't stand Annie, just so I could feel like my old self, be in my old life again.

Maybe Sam was avoiding Caro. I leaned my head back against the sofa and looked around and saw Joe talking to Sabrina by the food table. Sabrina was smiling and using her hands a lot, which meant she was seriously involved in the conversation. They were probably talking about the farm. I tried to pay attention to the story Annie was now telling, something about what an idiot someone was, but I found myself looking around again. Joe and Sabrina were still deep in conversation, but this time, they were sitting against the wall, and Joe had just offered Sabrina a bowl of chips he'd commandeered off the table.

Wait a minute! Sabrina was Joe's mystery dream girl! All that time he could have flirted with her at the farm and he'd been too shy and unsure of himself to say a word. To *Sabrina*!

I heard Sabrina's unmistakable nervous-girl laugh, the one she couldn't help when she felt out of her league. When she *did* care.

"Oh. My. God," Fergie snapped.

I followed her gaze to the front door.

Avery had arrived—with Tate.

"Oh no she didn't," Fergie said, staring Avery up and down.

Avery was all smiles. People were noticing her for sure. There was a lot of "What was your name again?" and "Aren't you in my French class?"

"She is so dead," Caro whispered.

Avery, looking absolutely gorgeous with her chic new hair and perfect makeup, was wearing Fergie's black minidress and Caro's strappy sandals that tied up the ankles.

Oh no she didn't was right. What was she thinking?

"Awww, the poor thing," Caro said very loudly, her eyes on Avery. "She's wearing the sandals I gave to Goodwill. And, Fergie, isn't that the dress you donated to Girls in Need?"

"Oh, wow, yes, it is," Fergie said. Loudly. "I guess she's in need."

I closed my eyes and counted to five. "Fergie, let it go," I whispered.

"Yeah, Fergie. Let. It. Go" was Tate's unhelpful response.

Avery's face fell for just a second, but her recovery was award-worthy. "Sorry, girls, but I just bought this yesterday. We all make mistakes, though." And then she took Tate's hand and led him through the party— which parted for them.

"Omigod, she is so dead!" Fergie exclaimed. "I'm going to personally kill her."

"I'll take care of her," Caro said. Then she eyed me. "Wow, thank you, Madeline. Good work."

"I told her not to wear your stuff!" I said. "She promised."

"Well, she didn't make good on her promise,"

Caro snapped. "And now she's going to wish she had. And what was that bit about letting it go, Madeline? Were you actually telling us to shut up? Were you actually coming to that loser dead girl's defense?"

All the girls sitting near us were staring at me.

My stomach turned over. I felt like I was going to throw up at any second. Everything was blowing up in my face. What was I supposed to do?

"I—I tried to help them, that's all. Don't blame me for what someone else does, Caro."

"Whatever," Caro said.

"Yeah, whatever," Fergie added.

And then a look passed between them.

"What are we whatevering?" Selena asked nervously as she arrived back with a plate of crudités, her gaze darting from me to Caro and to Fergie. "What did I miss?"

"Everything," I said, and slipped into the crowd, desperate to find a bathroom, close the door, and breathe.

Chapter 18

I went in search of Avery, but the party was so crowded I couldn't find her. Sam's backyard abutted a river, which people, mainly couples, were walking to and from along a cobblestoned path. Perhaps Avery and Tate were sitting on the river-bank, holding hands, and Tate was telling her not to worry about Caro and Fergie.

She should worry.

What was she thinking to pull something like that? To go up against Caro Alexander in such a public way?

What would have possessed Avery to show up in Caro's and Fergie's clothes, with the guy Fergie wanted? Not that she knew that Fergie had a crush on Tate. But why would she wear their clothes when I specifically told her not to? When she'd told us she was wearing a cute outfit she'd bought just for the party?

As the cliché said: I'd created a monster.

Maybe Avery was naive and really didn't understand the ramifications of what she'd done—crossing Caro Alexander, crossing Fergie, basically spitting on me—and she just didn't get how girls like Caro operated. How they ruled.

Or maybe she did. Maybe she had been brilliant and calculated.

What I wasn't sure about was whether she'd used me. Or whether I cared. Because I admired her. She *had* been brilliant. Avery had gone up against them and walked away triumphant—with the guy she wanted. The guy Fergie wanted.

And Caro would destroy her.

I didn't even know what I wanted to say to Avery. Maybe just *Why?* Or *Was it your plan all along? To find an in and then try to claw your way to the top?*

I headed back inside and tried to get to the bathroom so I could hide for a few minutes, but there was a line.

"Hey."

I turned around and there was Sam, with two bottles of iced tea. I wanted to grab his hand and run back outside and down that path to the river, to a spot without anyone nearby, and sit with him. I didn't even want to talk. I just wanted to feel him beside me.

He was about to say something when Caro was suddenly standing behind him, pressed up against him, her arms around his neck.

"I am soooo hot," she said. "Glad you're back with that drink," she added, taking one of the bottles. Then she took his hand and led him to the sofas. Instead of sitting down next to her, he walked over to the iPod dock that sat on a bookshelf. "Sam, it is so nice that you invited the interns you work with at Madeline's parents' farm," Caro said. She got up and started giving him a neck massage. "They really seem to be having a great time. I never see them out anywhere, so they must be really happy you included them."

He turned around and glanced at her. "That's nice of you to say."

"I'm *much* nicer than anyone gives me credit for," she said, gently raking her nails along the back of his neck.

I couldn't watch. I doubted he'd suddenly start making out with her, but either way, I couldn't stand watching them another second. I glanced around to check in on the interns. Joe and Sabrina were still sharing chips. Elinor had somehow become the ice girl and was dropping cubes into people's cups, her smile huge.

And then . . . disaster.

Shivers pinged their way up my spine.

Ceej was talking to Elinor. Really talking. Looking-deeply-into-her-eyes talking. Suddenly-taking-her-hand-and-leading-her-upstairs talking.

What was going on? Ceej was a jerk. And he wasn't suddenly falling for Elinor Espinoza. It was a setup. It had to be. Avery looked hot these days and acted like Caro and Fergie, so I had no doubt that Tate's interest was real. But Ceej's in Elinor? No.

And there was no way he was the guy she was crushing on. But attention from a hotshot like Ceej would turn Elinor's head.

I watched him take his cell phone from his back pocket, press something—like the *camera ready* button—and then slide it back into his pocket. Behind him, Elinor had a smile of nervous anticipation on her face. She'd never been kissed before.

No doubt he planned to take pictures of her with his cell phone and then send them all over school. I glanced at Fergie on the sofa. Was she behind this? She was deep in conversation with Annie, not gleefully watching Ceej lead Elinor to her doom. Ceej and his jerk friends probably planned it alone.

I raced up the stairs and grabbed her hand as she was about to follow Ceej into a bedroom. "Elinor, can I talk to you?"

She glanced from Ceej to me. "Um, okay."

"No problem," he said, waggling his eyebrows at her. "I'll be waiting for you right here."

I shot him a dirty look, then took her hand and led her back downstairs. "He's a jerk, Elinor. I don't want to be mean here, but he is totally setting you up."

The year before, Ceej had brought the usually shy Sandler twins to a room upstairs and gotten them to take off their shirts on the pretense of a biology assignment about whether identical twins had identical breasts. Everyone at Freeport Academy got to see that they did. Ceej had gotten into serious trouble—so serious that I couldn't believe he'd pull the same stupid stunt again. The Sandler twins transferred to Freeport High School.

She stared at me. "Why can't you believe for a second that a cute guy would go for me?" Tears sprang to her eyes.

I glanced at Elinor and let out a deep breath. I gently rubbed her arms. "I'm really sorry, Elinor. If it were any other guy . . . Sam or Jackson or Mike . . . ," I said, eyeing guys nearby. "But Ceej? He's got a mean soul. I just don't trust him not to hurt you in a very bad way."

Her shoulders slumped and she closed her eyes. "Me either. I mean, I've been the target of his jokes and name-calling for years. I just thought . . ." A tear slid down her face.

"You just thought that because you look amazing and worked so hard that maybe he noticed?" I asked.

Elinor nodded, mascara running down her cheeks.

"You know what, Elinor?" I said. "I'm ready to go home." At her hiccup, I added, "I'll tell Joe we're going. But he'll probably want to stay." Through the sliding glass doors, I could see Joe and Sabrina heading for the path to the river.

I glanced back at Caro and Fergie on the sofa, Annie and Selena sitting at their feet. They looked like a coven of witches casting a spell. I had no idea what they had planned for Avery. And I didn't really want to find out. Avery had said to me loud and clear tonight that she could take care of herself. But she had no idea what she was up against.

And there was no way she could go up against the Mosts and survive the rest of the school year.

I told Elinor I'd meet her outside, then headed to the sofas.

Caro was laughing. "Madeline, you're just in time to hear how we're going to ruin the life of the total

187

bitch you created. By lunch period on Monday, she'll wish she never crossed us."

I took a deep breath. "I was just coming over to say goodbye. This night has given me a total migraine."

"Oh please, Madeline. Stop being so sickly sweet. It doesn't suit you. And James has been asking where you are."

I stared at Caro. "I have to go."

"Whatever," she said.

"What are we whatevering now?" Selena and Annie asked in unison.

I glanced around for Sam, and there he was, talking to a couple of junior lacrosse players.

Once again, it was Sam I wished I could talk to. Sam I wished I could tell everything to. Sam I wished would hold me until I felt better. Not that feeling better seemed possible.

I sat in my kitchen, totally alone, eating red grapes and staring out at the pasture. Some cows stared at me, then went back to grazing. My mom and Mac were in their bedroom, watching an old movie. Sabrina wasn't home, which meant she was still busy getting her first boyfriend.

I'd eaten practically a pound of grapes when my

sister came in. She was glowing. Who knew that Joe could make a girl glow?

"Don't tell anyone," she said, bursting into a giggle, "but I think I'm seriously in like!"

I laughed. "Joe?"

She nodded. "Where the hell has he been hiding all my life? Oh, wait, I actually know the answer. He's been right here the whole time. Isn't that crazy?"

"He just needed some help in coming out of his shell," I said. "Grape?"

She popped one into her mouth. "I guess whatever you were helping the interns with worked. He went from too shy to talk to me to totally making me like him."

I glanced at her. "So you don't think what I did, giving them advice and tips and makeovers, was stupid and shallow?"

"A little shallow. But I have to say, the results are excellent."

"You didn't have to change, though," I pointed out. "You stayed exactly the same. And a guy who has had a huge secret crush on you forever did all this for *you*—went in with Avery and Elinor to pay me, changed his look, changed the way he acts and talks to people."

"*I* don't think there's anything wrong with me,"

she said. "That's the difference between me and a lot of other people. Including the asshats who try to get me down or put me on the Not list or call me Farmer Brown in the halls. I like how I look. And I had no problem with the way Joe used to look. I just never talked to him because he was so shy and kept to himself."

"Not anymore. I guess you have a boyfriend."

She smiled.

"So I have all the money I need to get to Dad's wedding," I said. "But I don't even know if I want to go anymore. Dad hasn't e-mailed me back in two days about what day I should fly in. Thom doesn't even return my texts anymore. The only reason to go is to—" I stopped and slumped over the table, my head in the crook of my elbow.

"To what?"

"To get away from my friends."

"Your friends are everywhere," she said. "There are girls like that in every school. If you move to California, you'll just get sucked into the new crowd of jerk popular girls."

I let out a deep breath. "So what am I supposed to do?"

"That I can't help you with. But I can tell you what Aunt Darcy would tell you. You're just supposed to be you."

• • •

Surprise, surprise. My dad finally got back to me.

> *Sweetsies, Tiffs and I are so happy you want to come, but I feel terrible that you'll be spending your own money to fly out. I wish I had the extra to cover it, honey. It's going to be such a small wedding that honestly, you'll feel like you're there if you watch the video. But if you do want to come, you could fly in the night before and try to sleep on the plane. Let me know what you decide. Love to you and Sabrina. —Dad*

How touching. He really *didn't* care whether I came to his wedding. Just like Sabrina had said. He almost deserved for me to fly out and tell him I was moving in. That would ruin his perfect little life with *Tiffs*. I had the date; I had the money. And I had the Web browser open on my computer to CheapTickets.com. I sat there, staring at the lowest-priced airline reservations from Portland, Maine, to Los Angeles, California. A one-way ticket was now $402.39, if I flew at 6 a.m. and connected twice.

I hovered over the *purchase tickets* button but couldn't click it.

To: CaroA@maine.com
From: MadGirl@maine.com

Did I miss anything after I left?
Like did you and Sam hook up? —M

No response.

Chapter 19

The whispering began in homeroom on Monday morning. Not about me. About Avery Kennar.

"Omigod, did you know that Avery Kennar has a baby and passes it off as her little sister? That's why she had to move here. So no one would know it was her kid!"

"You can't tell anyone this, but Avery Kennar has herpes. Someone overheard her filling a prescription at Rite Aid."

"The guy who got her pregnant wasn't even the guy who gave it to her. Can you believe she's such a slut?"

"The baby has herpes now because of her. Omigod, that is so sad!"

I heard variations of both those rumors all morning. Tate "confirmed" that Avery had herpes and that he'd found out in the "nick of time" in a bedroom at

Sam's party. "Dude, I was like one inch away from doing her when I saw the skeevy outbreak."

Since it came out of Tate's mouth and everyone saw him and Avery together at Sam's party, Avery and her herpes were now fact. The baby rumor was believed to be only 90 percent true, since no one knew if she even had a little sister in the first place.

At lunch, Fergie said, "I wonder which school Avery will transfer to. Maybe she'll just go to the public high school. She'll probably change her name."

Caro winked at Tate.

Bitch. Avery had tried to take Caro and Fergie down, and Caro had more than destroyed her—Caro had made Avery disappear. Avery wasn't in English class that morning. She'd probably heard the rumors in homeroom and fled.

I wondered what Caro had promised Tate to get him to betray a girl he'd obviously liked.

"Did she ever return my shoes?" Caro asked me.

I stared at her. "You want them back?"

"It's just the principle," Caro said before snapping an edamame pod in half.

"Yeah, it's the principle," Fergie repeated like a good little sidekick. Like a sheep.

Caro had been cool since the party. She'd picked me up that morning, same as always. Met me between classes. But she was distant. I'd asked if she'd gotten my text Saturday night and again asked what had happened between her and Sam at his party, but she had said that she'd decided not to kiss and tell anymore, that it was in bad taste.

I was dying.

Had they hooked up? Sam wasn't around at lunch, because he was on some sports committee that met then and they got to eat catered food. And after English class, Sam had left without even looking my way.

They were probably together. The new It Couple.

"So, Madeline," Fergie said as she clicked open her compact, "I assume you're sitting with me and Annie and Selena at the Lobster Claw Teen Queen Pageant and not with the farm freak's cheering committee. Does she even have any friends? She'll probably get laughed off the stage. Or booed. Poor thing."

"Of course she'll sit with you guys," Caro said, staring at me, snapping another edamame.

I had to get out of there. Away from Caro. Just away.

And there was someone I wanted to see.

I had study period after lunch, so I got a library pass and then snuck out to Avery's house. Her mom answered the door and said Avery had come home sick from school and it was so nice that I'd come to see how she was feeling.

I knew how she was feeling.

I knocked on her door, and she called, "It's open, Mom."

I opened it and poked my head in. "It's me."

She practically jumped—and then burst into tears.

I walked over to her bed and sat down on the edge. "Avery, what the hell were you thinking?" I handed her a tissue from the box that was already on her bed.

"I just thought I could be one of you guys," she said, her eyes red-rimmed from crying. "If I looked the part, if I had the attention of one of the cool guys—you know, just like you did it. But Caro still wouldn't talk to me at school. Neither would her little friends. So I figured I'd make a total scene and work my way in by being totally fierce."

"'Fierce' is a good word for it, actually."

"Do you hate me?" she asked.

"Nope. I actually admire you, Avery. What you did was brilliant and took guts. They might have blasted you today, but you blasted them first. You showed them up."

"Yeah, well, now I have herpes and a kid."

I squeezed her hand. "I'll take care of that, Avery. I used to be really well known at school for giving advice and tips and actually talking to people. I'm going to write an editorial for the school paper. About how crazy it is what people will do for popularity. Even me. And I'm going to say that you were trying to fit in and some girls got jealous and started very nasty rumors about you. Rumors that aren't true."

She sat up. "You'd do that? Seriously?"

"Seriously."

"Because you hate your friends and don't care if they ever talk to you again? Because they won't, I assume."

I shrugged. "Don't know and don't care anymore. That's the cool thing about what you did, Avery. You didn't care about what some mean girls thought about you. You did what you wanted. Fergie likes Tate? So what? He's single and isn't into her, obviously. So you went for him."

Like I'd been afraid to do with Sam. And I'd lost him to Caro, who thought I was a big drip now anyway.

I stayed at Avery's for the next hour, totally blowing off American government. We talked and talked and talked, about who we used to be, who we'd become, who we wanted to be. We had a lot in common.

"Oh, and I'll apologize to your parents for taking up an internship at the farm," she said. "I really hate that place. No offense. I only took the spot to try to get close to you and Sam."

I smiled. "I figured."

She let out a deep breath. "I know it's time to let go of the fake stuff and just be who I really am. Though I am going to fake a fever with a hot thermometer and use makeup to look pale until that newspaper comes out. No way am I going to school before that."

I smiled. "I'm going to let go of the fake too. And I know where I have to begin."

Chapter 20

The next night, I lay on my bed, staring at the sliver of moonlight against the dark ceiling of my room. It was just past ten o'clock. I called Thom. And he actually answered. His voice didn't send shivers down my back or make my stomach feel all warm and goopy. It was just nice to hear.

"Thom, I think I already know the answer. . . . I shouldn't spend $402 on an airline ticket to California, right?"

"Madeline, I—"

"You can tell me, Thom. You have a new girl-friend, right?"

"I didn't mean for it to happen. Maddie, I really tried. But there was this girl who really understood about having a long-distance relationship, because she'd had one, and it hadn't worked out, and . . .

now things have gotten—I'm sorry, Madeline. I should have said something."

"It's okay, Thom. Honestly, I'm glad you're happy."

"That means a lot. Thanks. You know, I feel like a jerk for even saying this, but can we be friends? I mean, I know we won't have a lot of reason to keep up, but you'll always mean a lot to me, Madeline."

I smiled. It was a bittersweet goodbye. "Me too."

"Say hi to everyone for me, okay?"

"I will."

And then he said goodbye and was *really* gone.

Saturday morning, I sent my dad a quick reply to his e-mail, saying that he was right and I'd just watch the video. I'd let go of that. I'd let go of Thom. And I needed to let Sam go too. He was with Caro now. But I didn't want things to be weird between me and Sam. I glanced out my window to see if he was around, and there he was, in front of a cow stall in the barn, managing to look gorgeous with a grooming brush in his hand. I slipped into my Wellies and headed outside. It was a sunny morning, so bright that I had to shield my eyes.

"Hey," he said, taking off his sunglasses.

"Hey."

Don't cry, I told myself. Just make things okay and walk away.

"So, Thom and I just officially broke up. I was the last to know, apparently."

"You okay?" he asked, brushing away flies from the cow.

I lifted my face to the warm June sunshine. "Yeah. It's not like I didn't know deep down. I mean, he's been blowing me off since the first week he left. But it's so official. Two years of my life over, just like that. I guess that's why I held on to hope for so long."

"Hope's good, Madeline. Hope is everything. Even when it's blown to bits."

"Well, that's how I feel. Blown to bits. Not because of Thom. Because of everything."

He stopped brushing and stared at the ground. "Me too. Caro told me, okay?"

"Told you what?"

He resumed brushing. Harder than before, which the cow seemed to like. "That you and James are together now."

That bitch! "Sam, I don't even like James as a person. We're *not* together. We've never been together."

"So she lied?"

201

I sighed. "Look, I don't want to make things weird between you and Caro. I'm happy for you guys if you're happy together."

"Me and Caro, together? Huh?"

"Aren't you together?"

He raised an eyebrow. "I don't even like *her* as a person."

That hope that had been blown to bits restored itself. A burst of happiness shot up every inch of my body. "You and Caro didn't hook up? She's not your girlfriend?"

"There's nothing about Caro Alexander I like, Madeline. I've heard some really mean stuff come out of Caro's mouth. Yeah, she's beautiful. But it's not enough."

And then we were standing closer together. Closer. Closer. And then we were kissing.

"Come to the Spring Fling dance with me," he whispered in my ear.

He kissed me again before I could answer.

"I'd love to," I said. And kissed him back.

Chapter 21

I found out Sam and I kissed for the first time on his sixteenth birthday. I wanted to get him a little present, so after breakfast, I grabbed my messenger bag and headed downtown, figuring that some shopping would perk me up and give me time to think. The early June air was warm, yet not humid, and the breeze felt amazing on my face as I pedaled down Flying Point Road toward town.

I rode to The Mangy Moose, which had really fun stuff in it, like cool umbrellas and great T-shirts. I found the perfect T-shirt for Sam and had it wrapped. As I was heading back, knowing I had to hurry to get ready for the pageant, I noticed the store Elinor had mentioned on a side street. Retro Girl. I wasn't into vintage stuff, so I'd never been in there. But I could see a hot pink dress in the window.

I leaned my bike against a fire hydrant and

walked over to check out the dress. It was really cool, like something a movie star from the forties would wear. I glanced at the price tag: $425.00. Below the price, in large red letters, it said, It's *silk*, people.

I stood there and stared at that dress and knew what I was going to do with all that money Elinor and Joe and Avery had paid me. And twenty-five dollars of my own.

I rode to Elinor's house with my messenger bag slung across my torso and the dress over my shoulder, against my back. Riding with one hand wasn't easy, but at least Elinor lived only a few minutes away.

I rang the bell and waited.

Elinor pulled open the door. Her hair looked great—smooth, shiny ringlets. But her dress? Not so much. It was an ill-fitting off-white one that was either too long or too short. It ended midcalf. "Hi," she said, clearly surprised.

"I have a present for you," I said, handing her the dress bag.

She stared at the red calligraphy across the bag: *Retro Girl*. "What's this?"

"Open it," I said.

She slid down the zipper, and the hot pink

flower appeared. She gasped and stared from the dress to me and back to the dress.

"But—"

"But it's time for you to change out of that and slip into this," I said.

Her hand flew to her mouth. "I can't believe you did this, Madeline. This dress cost even more than I paid you."

"Okay, so my gift back to you, then."

Her lip began to tremble. "I'm really, really, really touched. Thank you," she said, tears pooling in her eyes.

She was about to bawl, so I gave her a quick hug and told her I'd see her at the pageant.

And then I rode home, feeling better than I had in a long time.

That afternoon, Caro won the Lobster Claw Teen Queen Pageant for the third year in a row. Wearing a demure pink dress and sandals she would normally dismiss as "so middle school," she sang that old Whitney Houston song about how children were our future. She smiled sweetly—for an hour and a half. And she read her completely fake essay with feeling, even tearing up when she got to the part about the importance of teens volunteering in the community and helping those less fortunate.

Elinor, in her gorgeous hot pink dress, read a passage about the importance of imagination from her favorite book, *Anne of Green Gables*, and placed third. Which meant she beat out five other girls. Which meant she was jumping up and down with complete and utter joy.

"For a farm freak, Smelinor wasn't half bad," Fergie said as we got up from the hard metal folding chairs. "I expected her to stand there and burst into tears like she did in Latin last month. And I like her dress. I can't believe I like it, but I do. It's so forties glam."

I smiled. "She's worked really hard on her confidence. And look how smooth and shiny her ringlets are. She's totally gotten rid of the frizz." She still wore the purple glasses, because she loved them. But overall, she looked eccentric and arty instead of just plain weird. And she looked happy. Really happy.

Fergie, Selena, and Annie went to congratulate Caro. I said I'd catch up and went over to where Elinor was hugging and kissing her relatives.

"Third place!" Elinor trilled, showing me her ribbon and plaque. "My stepmother is so impressed." She leaned close. "She'll be off my back forever!"

"Congratulations!" I told her. "I'm so happy for you."

"I can't tell you what a boost this dress gave

me," she said, staring down at it. "I felt amazing up there wearing it. I felt like the homecoming queen or something."

Her relatives pulled her over to take pictures. She smiled huge smiles, twirling around in her gorgeous hot pink dress with her ribbon and plaque clutched against her chest.

Good for you, Elinor.

Caro was posing onstage as a photographer snapped pictures for the local newspaper. The pageant sponsor handed her a giant fake check.

I headed over to where Fergie, Selena, and Annie were taking pictures too.

"I just had a total moment," Fergie said to me. "Like, this is really a big deal for Smelinor. But for Caro, it's just another Saturday. I mean, of course she won. She's won every year she's been eligible, and she'll win the next two pageants. Like, where's the *challenge*? Every year, I have to constantly reinvent myself on a style level, keeping up with trends and whatnot. Caro just has to be beautiful— like *that'll* ever change." She glanced at me. "Omigod, don't tell her I said that."

I smiled. "I won't."

"Then again," Fergie added, "Caro could get fat or something. Or run over by a truck and be totally deformed and scarred. You never know."

Wishful thinking, Fergie?

"Oh, and, Madeline, I'd watch out if I were you. Caro is on the warpath about something to do with you, but she wouldn't tell me what."

Sam, no doubt.

"And, sorry, but she told me to tell you you're not invited to her celebration lunch at Yum's."

What a shock.

"So I heard you and Sam were seen making out in your front yard," Caro said on the phone that night. "But of course it's not true. I mean, Madeline Echols making out with Sam when she knows I like him? Impossible. She'd never do such a bitchy, dirty thing to her supposed friend."

Whoa. And who the hell was spying on me and Sam, anyway? Did Caro have secret-agent binoculars or something? Or maybe one of the summer interns who were having orientation sessions saw us and passed it on? Someone going by in a car probably saw us and the gossip train began.

"Bitchy and dirty? You mean like telling Sam I hooked up with James? That we were a couple now?"

"Don't compare the two, Madeline. Please."

"Caro, I—"

"Whatever," she snapped. "I don't care about

your explanations. I just want to know if it's true. Were you making out with Sam?"

It was time to stand up to Caro Alexander. "Yes, I was."

She hung up.

I really hoped I wouldn't have herpes or a baby the next morning at school.

Chapter 22

Monday, I waited for Mandy's car, as always, not expecting it. But there it was.

Caro lowered the window and said, "I heard another rumor that I swore to Fergie could not possibly be true. That you're going to the Spring Fling dance with Sam. Isn't that hilarious?"

Fergie burst into maniacal laughter. "It's so funny that it's not. Omigod, Caro, there is no way Madeline would screw you like that."

They wouldn't stab me or scratch my eyes out with Mandy watching, would they?

"Yes. He asked me and I said yes."

Caro stared at me, the angelic blue eyes ice cold. "There's a code, Madeline. You're aware of it. You don't go after the guy your friend likes. Every girl in the universe knows that rule and lives by it."

"Every girl," Fergie agreed. "I mean, come on, Madeline."

"I didn't mean to fall for him, Caro. You *know* that."

"I don't know anything about you anymore, Madeline. I just know you're *out*. And by the way, I want back *everything* I gave you. Every shirt, every necklace, every pair of shoes." She wrinkled her nose. "Ick, the smell here is revolting."

Then she raised the window and the car pulled away, the wheels spraying me with a dust of dirt and pebbles.

Sabrina and Elinor, who had the early shift that morning, were staring at me.

Oh no. I'd forgotten that Elinor had a huge crush on Sam too.

"Elinor, I'm—"

"Lucky," she said with a big smile. "Sam's a great guy. And amazingly gorgeous."

Huh? "You're not upset?"

She twirled a ringlet. "About?"

"I know you like him, Elinor."

"Not in a *real* way," she said. "I mean, I like him, but it's a crush like I'd have on a rock star or a movie star. Sam and I don't speak the same language."

"So do you think I was wrong for breaking the girl code?"

"You're asking me?"

I nodded. "I value your opinion." And it was true. I did.

"If you want to know how I really feel, I think Caro is pure evil. There is no girl code with a girl like her. There's only her evil code."

I couldn't help laughing. "I guess that makes me feel a little better."

She grinned. "So did I mention I have a date to the Spring Fling? With someone who does speak my language. He told me he loves my hair—when it gets all frizzy from the rain too!"

Frizz puffs and all. I gave her a hug. "Have an amazing time," I said as the big yellow school bus pulled to a noisy stop in front of us. I'd get the scoop later on who he was.

"Oh, I will," she said, and took a jump—but just a little, well-deserved one.

There were no rumors. Nothing was written about me on the bathroom walls. No one stared at me and whispered.

Life was completely the same at Freeport Academy that day. But it wouldn't be for much longer.

The piece I'd written for the *Freeport Academy Buzz* was coming out that day. Perfect timing, since I still had my standing for another few days, until the new Most and Not lists came out. And Avery would be coming back to school the next day.

"Great editorial," someone said to me, holding up the paper.

> My name is Madeline Echols. I was at the party that started some nasty and untrue rumors about my friend Avery Kennar. I just want to state for the record that none of it is true.
> —Madeline Echols

I'd planned to go on and on about popularity and how it could corrupt people and wasn't worth it. But I'd decided to keep the piece short and sweet and to the point.

"I knew it," was the refrain I heard around school immediately.

"You're such a stupid bitch."

I turned around and there was Caro, glaring at me. Fergie and the hangers-on were right behind her, looking nervous. She had a copy of the newspaper in her hand. "Whatever. Do you really think I care about that loser? You two deserve each other." And then she walked away, Fergie and the girls trailing her.

For the next week, I didn't sit with Caro and Fergie at lunch, didn't meet them between classes. Fergie didn't seek me out, and I didn't press it with her. Caro's friendship meant too much to her.

I'd put everything Caro had ever given me, two years' worth of castoffs, which actually didn't add up to all that much, into a huge shopping bag and then asked my mom to drive me over to her house to drop it off. I taped a big note—*Your stuff. M*—to the bag so that Mandy wouldn't mistake it for real garbage.

Though I wouldn't doubt Caro would ask Mandy to throw the bag away.

Sam and I made a pact to avoid each other at school. I didn't need more drama. He came over after school, and we went for long walks in the fields and I even helped him wash down Hermione, his favorite calf, too. Twice I burst into tears—once while we were talking about our English teacher, and another time while we were kissing on our rock.

"You'll be okay. It'll be okay," he kept assuring me.

I got ready for the dance at my house with Sabrina and Elinor and Avery, whose debut back at school (she'd faked a fever by pressing the thermometer in her hands and pretended to throw up every morning for the past week) went as planned. Everyone—well, except certain someones—said they'd known that all those rumors were false. And now Avery was famous, like she'd wanted to be.

Sabrina wore a dress for the first time in her life and actually let me put a little makeup on her face. "Is it too much?" she screeched after one coat of mascara. My sister? Totally pretty. And Elinor, with her long dark ringlets and her hot pink pageant dress, looked fabulous. Avery was decked out in a white dress with high-heeled sandals. And I was wearing the very first dress I'd bought in Rome, just a simple pale pink sheath, with my favorite cool necklace.

My mom and Mac were blown away by the transformations. Especially Sabrina's. My mom was tearing up so much she couldn't hold the camera straight, so Mac ended up snapping the pictures— like a hundred of them. And then Mac drove us all to the Freeport Academy gym, where the Spring Fling dance was held.

Joe, looking quite handsome in a black dress shirt, was waiting for Sabrina in front. And there was Sam, waiting for me.

"Maybe we should just skip it," I whispered to him, a balmy breeze ruffling my hair. "We could walk to the beach and just sit and talk."

"Or we could go in," he said, taking my hand.

So we went. The gym was packed, since it was a school-wide dance.

"Don't even look around for them," he said, putting his hands around my waist and leading me into a slow dance.

I slipped my arms around his neck and closed my eyes, but until I knew where Caro and Fergie were, I'd feel like a bucket of pig's blood might splash on my head at any moment. I glanced around. They were easy to spot. With her long blond hair, Caro looked very dramatic in a sleeveless black dress. And Fergie, as always, was fashion forward. She was slow-dancing with Tate, her head against his shoulder. And Caro was being twirled around by a gorgeous junior who was captain of the baseball team.

Sam and I slow-danced to two more songs, and between the music and the feel of his arms around me, I relaxed. Until I went to the restroom. One minute, I was washing my hands and freshening my lip gloss, and the next, Caro and Fergie had me surrounded.

Caro began brushing her hair. "Fergie," she said, "I just realized that the Not list will be decided tomorrow. I wonder if anyone new and unexpected will make the list this year."

"Yeah, I wonder," Fergie said, eyeing me. I couldn't tell if she was saying *Do something about the situation, idiot.* Or *You're toast.*

"I mean, now that some of the farm freaks have

216

actually improved," Caro added, "there's room for *others* who need help."

Whatever.

"Oh, by the way, *Maddie*," Caro said, "we've changed the rules this year. Everyone who made the Most list last year needs to be in the meeting to determine the Nots. To keep it fair and balanced. We're meeting in ten minutes on the quad."

"Fair and balanced?" I muttered through gritted teeth. "What is fair and balanced about judging people by the way they look?"

She laughed. "Oh, so you mean the entire country, who has had these Most and Best polls for generations, is wrong? If it's okay for me to be Most Beautiful, why isn't it okay for someone else to be Most Not Beautiful?"

"Because one is praise and the other is a put-down, Caro. Come on."

She stared at me. "No, you come on. To the meeting. The rule is firm. A few of us realized that since the Most polls aren't over, anyone can be voted for anything. I mean, a former Most can suddenly turn into a Not."

A threat. She knew I wouldn't go to that meeting. And she wanted me to sweat.

"Right. So you think Sam Fray, always voted Most Popular and Most Beautiful, will suddenly be voted Most in Need?"

"Maybe," she said. "In need of an attitude adjustment. Someone's played with his head. Sam has always been a nice guy. But you turned him into Mr. Save the Losers."

Then I walked away.

"You're fair game now," she called after me.

When I found Sam right where I'd left him, I took his hand. "Let's go out back. We can still hear the music but get away from the crowds."

"Sounds good to me," he said, leading us out.

Dusk finally falling into a beautiful summer night, we slow-danced on the grass, even to the fast songs. It felt like there was no one and nothing else in the world. No lists, no Caro and Fergie. Just me and Sam and possibilities.

"I give you permission to break up with me tomorrow," I whispered. "I'm probably going to end up on the Not list."

He pulled away from me. "I hope you're kidding. You do know me better, right?"

Tears pricked my eyes. "Yeah. I do. I'm just overwhelmed by everything. I don't know what to think about anything anymore."

He pulled me against him and caressed my hair. "Actually, if you do end up on the Not list, it might be a good thing."

"A good thing to be a Not?" I asked, staring at him.

He nodded. "Madeline Echols, gorgeous, funny, nice, smart, a Not? How can that possibly make sense? It'll completely destroy the power that list has, because no one will believe it."

"I hope you're right." How could I go from Most Popular to Most Not overnight? It would render the list meaningless. For me, anyway.

"I'm right," he assured me, then pulled me tighter against him.

Chapter 23

The Not list started making its way around the school during homeroom the next morning.

SOPHOMORE CLASS MOST NOTS

Most in Need of a Reality Check:
Madeline Echols & Jeff Parker

Most in Need of New Friends:
Madeline Echols & Simon Archweller

Most Changed into a Loser:
Madeline Echols & Avery Kennar

Most in Need of an Extreme Makeover:
Lauren Goddard & Mike Farraday (unibrow, bro)

Most in Need of a Stylist:
Penny Kerns & Mike Farraday

Most in Need of a Therapist:
Madeline Echols

Most in Need:
Madeline Echols

Most in Need of a Bodyguard:
Avery Kennar

The list went on, with names I didn't recognize—other than my own. And it didn't hurt a bit. Just like Sam had said it wouldn't.

They're not on the list, I realized, letting out a breath. Elinor and Joe weren't on the list. We'd done it.

Caro had probably tried her damnedest to get Elinor on the Not list. But she must have been overruled. And Avery's inclusion was kind of funny. She'd love it.

Caro Alexander, overruled. *I* loved it.

A girl I didn't know came up to me, a group of girls behind her. "Um, hi, um, can I just ask you something?"

"Sure," I said.

"Is this list a joke?" she asked, holding up the Not list. "I mean, I'm on it. But so are you."

"Yeah," I assured her. "It's a total joke. Don't pay any attention to it."

"See? I told you," another girl said, and when the bell rang, they all crumpled the lists and chucked them into the garbage can by the door.

As I walked to English, I could see the crowd parting ahead. Caro, Fergie, Selena, and Annie walked past me. None of them looked at me, but Fergie turned back for a second.

Caro was right about one thing. I was most in need of new friends.

My cell phone vibrated. A text from Elinor.

Even if I were on the Not list, I wouldn't be. Does that make sense? You're not on it either. —E

Yeah. It made a lot of sense.

All Most ballots were due to the office by noon the next day. Mrs. Farker, the school secretary, guarded the box where ballots, folded and stapled shut in front of her, were dropped through a narrow slot. You had to check your initials against her list before turning in your ballot. All this was because of a scam four years earlier, when one girl had received 317 votes for Most Popular, Most Beautiful, and Most Likely to Rule the World One Day, and there had been only 173 students in the class.

The Most list would be posted the following day after lunch.

I didn't vote. Neither did Sam.

SOPHOMORE CLASS POLL

Most Popular
Madeline Echols and Sam Fray

Most Beautiful
Caro Alexander and Sam Fray

Most Stylish
Fergie Ferragamo and CJ Marstow

Most Hot
Selena McFarland and Tate Belsh

Most Likely to Rule the World One Day
Avery Kennar and Tate Belsh

Most Brainy
Jen Bay and Devlin Murphy

Most Hilarious
Annie Haywood and Tate Belsh

Class Couple
Madeline Echols and Sam Fray

So.

What Happened Next

During the final few days of school, Caro did not start rumors about me. She didn't arrange to have me run over. She just pretended I didn't exist.

Fergie has waved at me the few times she's seen me when she hasn't been with Caro. But when she's with Caro, she ignores me. Right after it all happened, she e-mailed me: *I wish we could still be friends, but you broke the code.* There's no point in telling Fergie my side. First of all, there is no *there* there, as Sabrina loves to say about my former friends. And Fergie lives for Caro.

Sam is spending the summer working full-time at the farm. I, of course, am not. Avery and I are junior counselors at a day camp and have become really good friends with another girl, who just moved to Freeport and will be attending Freeport

Academy in the fall as a junior, just like us. We've told her *everything*. Leila is from New York City and is incredibly cool and stylish, but not in a high-fashion couture way. In a her-own-style way. Fergie will hate her.

Sabrina was voted Most in Need again in the junior-class Not polls. She didn't care again. She and Joe have decided they are Junior Class Couple.

Elinor's Spring Fling date turned into a boyfriend. She still has the occasional frizz puffs, but she traded in her glasses for contacts when the boyfriend told her she had the most beautiful eyes he'd ever seen.

My dad and Tiffany are expecting a baby. I'm really happy for him.

Avery and I have become very close.

Sam told me he loves me. I told him I love him.

Aunt Darcy sent me a huge "congratulations on the love thing" box of chocolates, no gross pink-cream centers. *To: Most You,* she'd written on the little card.

The Most Me. That is all I want to be.

Acknowledgments

First, this book would not *be* without the guidance
and brilliance (and incredible patience) of my editor, Wendy Loggia. Thank you, thank you, thank
you.

Big thanks to my agents, Alexis Hurley and Kim
Witherspoon at Inkwell Management.

The very kind owners of the Mitchell Ledge
Farm took time out of their busy schedule to sit
down and talk cows with me, and I appreciate it
very much! Thank you, Mary and Andy.

Oh, to have a trusted friend who is also an author! Thank you, Lee Nichols.

And as always, a big thank-you to my adorable,
amazing little guy, Max, a constant source of inspi-
ration.

Monica Moore

MELISSA SENATE is the author of eight other novels, including her debut for teens, *Theodora Twist*, hailed by *Teen People* as a "hot summer read" and by the *New York Post* as "realistically raw, yet endearing." A former editor of teen fiction in New York City, Melissa now lives on the coast of Maine, where *The Mosts* is set.